A Mere Accident

George Moore

Contents

A MERE ACCIDENT

BY

George Moore

A MERE ACCIDENT.
CHAPTER I

THREE hundred yards of smooth, broad, white road leading from Henfield, a small town in Sussex. The grasses are lush, and the hedges are tall and luxuriant. Restless boys scramble to and fro, quiet nursemaids loiter, and a vagrant has sat down to rest though the bank is dripping with autumn rain.

How fair a prospect of southern England! Land of exquisite homeliness and order; land of town that is country, of country that is town; land of a hundred classes all deftly interwoven and all waxing to one class—England. Land encrowned with the gifts of peaceful days—days that live in thy face and the faces of thy children.

See it. The outlying villas with their porches and laurels, the red tiled farm houses, and the brown barns, clustering beneath the wings of beautiful trees—elm trees; see the flat plots of ground of the market gardens, with figures bending over baskets of roots; see the factory chimney; there are trees and gables everywhere; see the end of the terrace, the gleam of glass, the flower vase, the flitting white of the tennis players; see the long fields with the long team ploughing, see the parish church, see the embowering woods, see the squire's house, see everything and love it, for everything here is England.

Three hundred yards of smooth, broad, white road, leading from Henfield, a small town in Sussex. It disappears in the woods which lean across the fields towards the downs. The great bluff heights can be seen, and at the point where the roads cross, where the tall trunks are listed with golden light, stands a large wooden gate and a small box-like lodge. A lonely place in a densely-populated county. The gatekeeper is blind, and his flute sounds doleful and strange, and the leaves are falling.

The private road is short and stony. Apparently space was found for it with difficulty, and it got wedged between an enormous holly hedge and a stiff wooden paling. But overhead the great branches fight upwards through a tortuous growth to the sky, and, as you advance, Thornby Place continues to puzzle you with its medley of curious and contradictory aspects. For as the second gate, which is in iron, is approached, your thoughts of rural things are rudely scattered by sight of what seems a London mews. Reason with yourself. This very urban feature is occasioned by the high brick wall which runs parallel with the stables, and this, as you pass round to the front of the house, is hidden in the clothing foliage of a line of evergreen oaks; continuing along the lawn, the trees bend about the house—a wash of Naples-yellow, a few sharp Italian lines and angles. To complete the sketch, indicate the wings of the blown rooks on the sullen sky.

But our purpose lies deeper than that which inspires a water-colour sketch. We must learn when and why that house was built; we must see how the facts reconcile its somewhat tawdry, its somewhat suburban aspect, with the richer and more romantic aspects of the park. The park is even now, though it be the middle of autumn, full of blowing green, and the brown circling woods, full of England and English home life. That single tree in the foreground is a lime; what a splendour of leafage it will be in the summer! Those four on the right are chestnuts, and those far away, lying between, us and the imperial downs, are elms; through that vista you can see the grand line, the abrupt hollows, and the bit of chalk road cut zig-zag out of the steep side. Then why the anomaly of Italian urns and pilasters; why not red Elizabethan gables and diamond casements?

Why not? Because at the beginning of the century, when Brighton was being built, fragments of architectural gossip were flying about Sussex, and one of these had found its way to, and had rested in, the heart of the grandfather of the present owner: in a simple and bucolic way he had been seized by a desire for taste and style, and the present building was the result. Therefore it will be well to examine in detail the house which young John Norton of '86 was so fond of declaring he could never see without becoming instantly conscious of a sense of dislike, a hatred that he was fond of describing as a sort of constitutional complaint which he was never quite free from, and which any view of the Rockery, or the pilasters of the French bow-window, or indeed of anything pertaining to Thornby Place, called at once into an active existence.

Thornby Place is but two stories high, and its spruce walls of Portland stone and ashlar work rise sheer out of the green sward; in front, Doric columns support a heavy entablature, and there are urns at the corners of the building. The six windows on the ground floor are topped with round arches, and coming up the drive the house seems a perfect square. But this regularity of structure has on the east side been somewhat interfered with by a projection of some thirty or forty feet—a billiard room, in fine, which during John's minority Mrs Norton had thought proper to add. But she had lived to rue her experiment, for to this young man, with his fretful craving for beauty and exactness of proportion, it is an ever present source of complaint; and he had once in a half humorous, half serious way, gone so far as to avail himself of the "eyesore," as he called it, to excuse his constant absence from home, and as a pretence for shutting himself up in his dear college, with his cherished Latin authors. It was partly for the sake of avenging himself on his mother, whose decisive practicality jarred the delicate music of a nature extravagantly ideal, that he so severely criticised all that she held sacred; and his strictures fell heaviest on the bow window, looking somewhat like a temple with its small pilasters supporting the rich cornice from which the dwarf vaulting springs. The loggia, he admitted, although painfully out of keeping with the surrounding country, was not wholly wanting in design, and he admired its columns of a Doric order, and likewise the cornice that like a crown encompasses the house. The entrance is under the loggia; there are round arched windows on either side, a square window under the roof, and the hall door is in solid oak studded with ornamental nails.

On entering you find yourself in a common white-painted passage, and on either side of the drawing-room and dining-room are four allegorical female heads: Spring, Summer, Autumn, and Winter. Further on is the hall, with its short polished oak stairway sloping gently to a balcony; and there are white painted pillars that support the low roof, and these pillars make a kind of entrance to the passage which traverses the house from end to end. England—England clear and spotless! Nowhere do you find a trace of dust or disorder. The arrangement of things is somewhat mechanical. The curtains and wall-paper in the bedrooms are suggestive of trades people and housemaids; no hastily laid aside book or shawl breaks the excessive orderliness. Every piece of furniture is in its appointed place, and nothing testifies to the voluntariness of the occupant, or the impulse prompted by the need of the moment. On the presses at the ends of the passages, where is stored the house linen, cards are hung bearing this inscription: "When washing the woodwork the servants are requested to use no soda without first obtaining permission from Mrs Norton." This detail was especially distasteful to John; he often thought of it when away, and it was one of the many irritating impressions which went to make up the sum of his dislike of Thornby Place.

Mrs Norton is now crying her last orders to the servants; and although dressed elaborately as if to receive visitors, she has not yet laid aside her basket of keys. She is in her forty-fifth year. Her figure is square and strong, and not devoid of matronly charm. It approves a healthy mode of life, and her quick movements are indicative of her sharp determined mind. Her face is somewhat small for her shoulders, the temples are narrow and high, the nose is long and thin, the cheek bones are prominent, the chin is small, but unsuggestive of weakness, the lips are pinched, the complexion is flushed, and the eyes set close above the long thin nose are an icy grey. Mrs Norton is a handsome woman. Her fashionably-cut silk fits her perfectly; the skirt is draped with grace and precision, and the glossy shawl with the long soft fringe is elegant and delightfully mundane. She raises her double gold eyeglasses, and, contracting her forehead, stares pryingly about her; and so fashionable is she, and her modernity is so picturesque, that for a moment you think of the entrance of a duchess in the first act of a piece by Augier played on the stage of the Francois.

Still holding her gold-rimmed glasses to her eyes, she descended the broad stairs to the hall, and from thence she went into the library. There are two small bookcases filled with sombre volumes, and the busts of Molière and Shakespeare attempt to justify the appellation. But there is in the character, I was almost going to say in the atmosphere of the room, that same undefinable, easily recognizable something which proclaims the presence of non-readers. The traces of three or four days, at the most a week, which John occasionally spent at Thornby Place, were necessarily ephemeral, and the weakness of Mrs Norton's sight rendered continuous reading impossible. Sometimes Kitty Hare brought a novel from the circulating library to read aloud, and sometimes John forgot one of his books, and a volume of Browning still lay on the table. The room was filled with shadow and mournfulness, and in a dusty grate the fire smouldered.

Between this room and the drawing-room, in a recess formed by the bow window, Mrs Norton kept her birds, and still peering through her gold-rimmed glasses, she examined their seed-troughs and water-glasses, and, having satisfied herself as to their state, she entered the drawing-room. There is little in this room; no pictures relieve the widths of grey colourless wall paper, and the sombre oak floor is spaced with a few pieces of furniture—heavy furniture enshrouded in grey linen cloths. Three French cabinets, gaudy with vile veneer and bright brass, are nailed against the walls, and the empty room is reflected dismally in the great gold mirror which faces the vivid green of the sward and the duller green of the encircling elms of the park.

Mrs Norton let her eyes wander, and sighing she went into the dining-room. The dining-room is always the most human of rooms, and the dining-room in Thornby Place, although allied to the other rooms in an absence of fancy in its arrangement, shows prettily in contrast to them with its white cloth cheerful with flowers and ferns. The floor is covered with a tightly stretched red cloth, the chairs are set in symmetrical rows; with the exception of a black clock there is no ornament on the chimney-piece, and a red cloth screen conceals the door used by the servants.

Mrs Norton walked with her quiet decisive step to the window, and holding the gold rimmed glasses to her eyes, she looked into the landscape as if she were expecting someone to appear. The day was grimy with clouds; mist had risen, and it hung out of the branches of the elms like a veil of white gauze. Withdrawing her eye from the vague prospect before her, Mrs Norton played listlessly with the tassel of one of the blinds. "Surely," she thought, "he cannot have been foolish enough to have walked over the downs such a day as this;" then, raising her glasses again she looked out at the smallest angle with the wall of the house, so that she should get sight of a vista through which any one coming from Shoreham would have to pass. Presently a silhouette appeared on the sullen sky. Mrs Norton moved precipitately from the window, and she rang the bell sharply.

"John," she said, "Mr Hare has been going in for one of his long walks. I see him now coming across the park. I am sure he has walked over the downs; if so he must be wet through. Have a fire lighted in Mr Norton's room, put up a pair of slippers for him: here is the key of Mr Norton's wardrobe; let Mr Hare have what he wants."

And having detached one from the many bunches which filled her basket, she went herself to open the door to her visitor. He was however still some distance away, and standing in the shelter of the loggia she waited for him, watched the vague silhouette resolving itself into colour and line. But it was not until he climbed the iron fence which separated the park from the garden grounds that the figure grew into its individuality. Then you saw a man of about forty, about the medium height and inclined to stoutness. His face was round and florid, and it was set with sandy whiskers. His white necktie proclaimed him a parson, and the grey mud with which his boots were bespattered told of his long walk. As is generally the case with those of his profession, he spoke fluently, his voice was melodious, and his rapid answers and his bright eyes saved him from appearing commonplace. In addressing Mrs Norton he used her Christian name.

"You are quite right, Lizzie, you are quite right; I shouldn't have done it: had I known what a state the roads were in, I wouldn't have attempted it."

"What is the use of talking like that, as if you didn't know what these roads were like! For twenty years you have been making use of them, and if you don't know what they are like in winter by this time, all I can say is that you never will."

"I never saw them in the state they are now; such a slush of chalk and clay was never seen."

"What can you expect after a month of heavy rain? You are wringing wet."

"Yes, I was caught in a heavy shower as I was crossing over by Fresh-Combe-bottom. I am certainly not in a fit state to come into your dining-room."

"I should think not indeed! I really believe if I were to allow it, you would sit the whole afternoon in your wet clothes. You'll find everything ready for you in John's room. I'll give you ten minutes. I'll tell them to bring up lunch in ten minutes. Stay, will you have a glass of wine before going upstairs?"

"I am afraid of spoiling your carpet."

"Yes, indeed! not one step further! I'll fetch it for you."

When the parson had drunk the wine, and was following the butler upstairs, Mrs Norton returned to the dining-room with the empty glass in her hand. She placed it on the chimney piece; she stirred the fire, and her thoughts flowed pleasantly as she dwelt on the kindness of her old friend. "He only got my note this morning," she mused. "I wonder if he will be able to persuade John to return home."

Mrs Norton, in her own hard, cold way, loved her son, but in truth she thought more of the power of which he was the representative than of the man himself: the power to take to himself a wife—a wife who would give an heir to Thornby Place. This was to be the achievement of Mrs Norton's life, and the difficulties that intervened were too absorbing for her to think much whether her son would find happiness in marriage; nor was it natural to her to set much store on the refining charm and the uniting influences of mental sympathies. Had she not passed the age when the sentimental emotions are liveliest? And the fibre was wanting in her to take into much account the whispering or the silence of passion.

Mrs Norton saw in marriage nothing but the child, and in the child nothing but an heir—that is to say, a male who would continue the name and traditions of Thornby Place. This would seem to indicate a material nature, but such a mis-apprehension arises from the common habit of confusing pure thought—thought which proceeds direct from the brain and lives uncoloured by the material wants of life—with instincts whose complexity often causes them to appear as mental potentialities, whereas they are but instincts, inherited promptings, and aversions more or less modified by physical constitution and the material forces of the life in which the constitution has grown up; and yet, though pure thought, that is to say the power of detaching oneself from the webs of life and viewing men and things from a height, is the rarest of gifts, many are possessed of sufficient intellectuality to enjoy with the brain apart from the senses. Mrs Norton was such an one. After five o'clock tea she would ask Kitty to read to her, and drawing her shawl about her shoulders, would readily abandon the intellectual side of her nature to the se-ductive charm of the romantic story of James of Scotland; and while to the girl the heroism and chivalry were a little clouded by the quaint turns of Rossetti's verse, to the woman these were added delights, which her quiet penetrating understanding followed and took instant note of.

"Were mother and son ever so different?" was the common remark. The artistic was the side of Mrs Norton's character that was unaffectedly kept out of sight, just as young John Norton was careful to hide from public knowledge his strict business habits, and to expose, perhaps a little ostentatiously, the spiritual impulses in which he was so deeply concerned: the subtle refinement of sacred places, from the mys-tery of the great window with its mitres and croziers to the sunlit path between the tombs where the children play, the curious and yet natural charm that attendance in the sacristy had for him, the arrangement of the large oak presses, wherein are stored the fine altar linen and the chalices, the distributing of the wine and water that were not for bodily need, and the wearing of the flowing surplices, the murmuring of the Latin responses that helped so wonderfully to enforce the impression of beautiful and refined life which was his, and which he lived beyond the gross influences of the wholly temporal life which he knew was raging almost but not quite out of hearing. But, however marked may be the accidental variations of character, hereditary instincts are irresistible, and in obedience to them John neglected nothing that concerned his pecuniary instincts. He was in daily communication with his agent, and the financial position of every farmer, and the state of every farm on his property, were not only known to him but were constantly borne in mind, and influenced him in that progressive ordering of things which marked the administration of his property. He was furnished quarterly with an account of all monies paid, to which were joined descriptive notes of each farm, showing what alterations the past three months had brought, and setting forth the agricultural intentions and abilities of the occupier.

John Norton waited the arrival of these accounts with a keen interest: they were a relish to his life; and without experiencing any revulsion of feeling, he would lay down a portfolio filled with photographs of drawings by Leonardo da Vinci—studies of drapery, studies of hands and feet, realistic studies of thin-lipped women and ecstatic angels with the light upon their high foreheads—and cheerfully, and even with a sense of satisfaction, he would untie the bald, prosaic roll of paper, and seating himself at his window overlooking the long terrace, he would add up the figures submitted to him, detecting the smallest arithmetical error, making note of the least delay in payment of any money due, and questioning the slightest overpayment for work done. The morning hours fled as he pursued his congenial task; and from time to time he would let his thoughts wander from the teasing computation of the money that would be required to make the repairs that a certain farmer had demanded, to the unworldly quiet of the sacristy; he would think, and his thoughts contained an evanescent sense of the paradox, of the altar linen he would have to fold and put away, and of the altar breads he would presently have to write to London for; and meanwhile his eyes would follow in delight the black figures of the Jesuits, who, with cassocks blowing and berrettas set firmly on their heads, walked up and down the long gravel walks reading their breviaries.

And living thus, half in the persuasive charm of ceremonial, half in the hard procession of account books, the last three years of John's life had passed. On coming of age he had spent a few weeks at Thornby Place, but the place, and especially the country, had appeared to him so grossly protestant—so entirely occupied with the material well-to-doness of life—that he declared he longed to breathe again the breath of his beloved sacristy, that he must away from that close and oppressive atmosphere of the flesh. Since then, with the exception of a few visits of a few days he had lived at Stanton College, writing to his mother not of the business which concerned his property, but of mental problems and artistic impulses. On business matters he never consulted her; but he thought it fortunate that she should choose to spend her jointure on Thornby Place, and so save him a great deal of expense in keeping up the house, which, although he disliked it with a dislike that had grown inveterate, he was still unwilling to allow to fall to ruins.

Mrs Norton, as has been said, was capable of understanding much in the abstract; so long as things, and ideas of things, did not come within the circle of her practical life, they were judged from a liberal standpoint, but so soon as they touched any personal consideration, they were judged by a moral code that in no way corresponded to her intellectual comprehension of the matter she so unhesitatingly condemned. But by this it must by no means be understood that Mrs Norton wore her conscience easily—that it was a garment that could be shortened or lengthened to suit all weathers. Our diagnosis of Mrs Norton's character involves no accusation of laxity of principle. Mrs Norton was a woman with an intelligence, who had inherited in all its primary force a code of morals that had grown up in the narrower minds of less gifted generations. In talking to her you were conscious of two active and opposing principles: reason and hereditary morality. I use "opposing," as being descriptive of the state of soul that would generally follow from such mental contradiction, but in Mrs Norton no shocking conflict of thought was possible, her mind being always strictly subservient to her instinctive standard of right and wrong.

And John had inherited the moral temperament of his mother's family, and with it his mother's intelligence, nor had the equipoise been disturbed in the transmitting; his father's delicate constitution in inflicting germs of disease had merely determined the variation represented by the marked artistic impulses which John presented to the normal type of either his father's or his mother's family. It would therefore seem that any too sudden corrective of defect will result in anomaly, and, in the case under notice, direct mingling of perfect health with spinal weakness had germinated into a marked yearning for the heroic ages, for the supernatural as contrasted with the meanness of the routine of existence. And now before closing this psychical investigation, and picking up the thread of the story, which will of course be no more than an experimental demonstration of the working of the brain into which we are looking, we must take note of two curious mental traits both living side by side, and both apparently negative of the other's existence: an intense and ever pulsatory horror of death, a sullen contempt and often a ferocious hatred of life. The stress of mind engendered by the alternating of these themes of suffering would have rendered life an unbearable burden to John, had he not found anchorage in an invincible belief in God, a belief which set in stormily for the pomp and opulence of Catholic ceremonial, for the solemn Gothic arch and the jewelled joy of painted panes, for the grace and the elegance and the order of hieratic life.

In a being whose soul is but the shadow of yours, a second soul looking towards the same end as your soul, or in a being whose soul differs radically, and is concerned with other satisfactions and other ideals, you will most probably find some part of the happiness of your dreams, but in intercourse with one who is grossly like you, but who is absolutely different when the upper ways of character are taken into account, there will be—no matter how inexorable are the ties that bind—much fret and irritation and noisy clashing. It was so with John Norton and his mother; even in the exercise of faculties that had been directly transmitted from one to the other there had been angry collision. For example:—their talents for business were identical; but while she thought the admirable conduct of her affairs was a thing to be proud of, he would affect an air of negligence, and would willingly have it believed that he lived independent of such gross necessities. Then his malady—for intense depression of the spirits was a malady with him—offered an ever-recurring cause of misunderstanding. How irritating it was when he lay shut up in his room, his soul looking down with murderous eyes on the poor worm that writhed out its life in view of the pitiless stars, and longing with a fierce wild longing to shake off the burning garment of consciousness, and plunge into the black happiness of the grave, to hear Mrs Norton on the threshold uttering from time to time admonitory remarks.

"You should not give way to such feelings, sir; you should not allow yourself to be unhappy. Look at me, am I unhappy? and I have more to bear with than you, but I am not always thinking of myself. . . . I am in fairly good health, and I am always cheerful! Why are you not the same? You bring it all upon yourself; I have no pity for you. . . . You should cease to think of yourself, and try to do your duty."

John groaned when he heard this last word. He knew very well what his mother meant. He should buy three hunters, he should marry. These were the anodynes that were offered to him in and out of season. "Bad enough that I should exist! Why precipitate another into the gulf of being?" "Consort with men whose ideal hovers between a stable boy and a veterinary surgeon;" and then, amused by the paradox, John, to whom the chase was evocative of forests, pageantry, spears, would quote some stirring verses of an old ballad, and allude to certain pictures by Rubens, Wouver-mans, and Snyders. "Why do you talk in that way?" "Why do you seek to make yourself ridiculous?" Mrs Norton would retort.

Smiling just a little sorrowfully, John would withdraw, and on the following day he would leave for Stanton College. And it was thus that Mrs Norton's temper scarred with deep wounds a nature so pale and delicate, so exposed that it seemed as if wanting an outer skin; and as Thornby Place appeared to him little more than a comprehensive symbol of what he held mean, even obscene in life, his visits had grown shorter and fewer, until now his absence extended to the verge of the second year, and besieged by the belief that he was contemplating priesthood, Mrs Norton had written to her old friend, saying that she wanted to speak to him on matters of great importance. Now maturing her plans for getting her boy back, she stood by the bare black mantel-piece, her head leaning on her hand. She uttered an exclamation when Mr Hare entered.

"What," she said, "you haven't changed your things, and I told you would find a suit of John's clothes. I must insist——"

"My dear Lizzie, no amount of insistance would get me into a pair of John's trousers. I am thirteen stone and a half, and he is not much over ten."

"Ah! I had forgotten, but what are you to do? Something must be done, you will catch your death of cold if you remain in your wet clothes. . . . You are wringing wet."

"No, I assure you I am not. My feet were a little wet, but I have changed my stockings and shoes. And now, tell me, Lizzie, what there is for lunch," he said, speaking rapidly to silence Mrs Norton, whom he saw was going to protest again.

"Well, you know it is difficult to get much at this season of the year. There are some chickens and some curried rabbit, but I am afraid you will suffer for it if you remain the whole of the afternoon in those wet clothes; I really cannot, I will not allow it."

"My dear Lizzie, my dear Lizzie," cried the parson, laughing all over his rosy skinned and sandy whiskered face, "I must beg of you not to excite yourself. I have no intention of committing any of the imprudences you anticipate. I will trouble you for a wing of that chicken. James, I'll take a glass of sherry, . . . and while I am eating it you shall explain as succinctly as possible the matter you are minded to consult me on, and when I have mastered the subject in all its various details, I will advise you to the best of my power, and having done so I will start on my walk across the hills. " "What! you mean to say you are going to walk home? . . . We shall have another downpour presently."

"Even so. I cannot come to much harm so long as I am walking, whereas if I drove home in your carriage I might catch a chill . . . It is at least ten miles to Shoreham by the road, while across the hills it is not more than six."

"Six! it is eight if it is a yard!"

"Well, perhaps it is; but tell me, I am curious to hear what you want to talk to me about. . . Something about John, is it not?"

"Of course it is, what else have I to think about; what else concerns middle-aged people like you and me but our children? Of course I want to talk to you about John. Something must be done, things cannot go on as they are. Why, it is nearly two years since he has been home. Oh, that boy is breaking my heart, and none suspects it. If you knew how it annoys me when the Gardiners and the Prestons congratulate me on having a son so well behaved. They know he looks after his property sharp enough, no drinking, no bad company, no debts. Ah! they little know. . . . I would much sooner he were wild and foolish: young men get over those kind of faults, but he will never get over his."

Mr Hare felt these views to be of a doubtful orthodoxy, but he did not press his opinion, and contented himself with murmuring gently that for the moment he did not see that John's faults were of a particularly aggravated character.

"You do not see that his faults should cause me any uneasiness! Perhaps it is very lucky he is not here, or you might encourage him in them. I suppose you think he is doing quite right in spending his life at Stanton College, aping a priest and talking about Gothic arches. Is it a proper thing to transact all his business through a solicitor, and never to see his tenants? Why does he not come and live at his own beautiful place? Why does he not take up his position in the county? He is not a magistrate. Why does he not get married? . . . he is the last; there is no one to follow him. But he never thinks of that—he is afraid that a woman might prove a disturbing influence in his life . . . . he feels that he must live in an atmosphere of higher emotions. That's the way he talks, and he is meditating, I assure you, a book on the literature of the Middle Ages, on the works of bishops and monks who wrote Latin in the early centuries. His mind, he says, is full of the cadences of that language. That's the way he writes. He never asks me about his property, never consults me in anything. Here is a letter I received yesterday. Listen:

"The poverty of spiritual life amid the western pagans could not fail to encourage the growth of new religious tendencies, An epoch of great spiritual activity had been succeeded by one of complete stagnation. A glance at the literary progress of Rome since Tiberius will show this emancipation from national and political considerations, the influence of cosmopolitanism gave to the best specimens of Latin prose of the silver age such riches and variety of substance and such individuality of expression, that Seneca and Tacitus and the letters of Pliny are marked with many modern characteristics. Form and language appear in these writers only as the instrument and the matter wherewith men of genius would express their intimate personality. Here antique culture rises above itself, but, mark you, at the expense of all that is proper to the Roman nation. Cosmopolitan Hellenism forces and breaks down the bars of classical traditions, and, weary of restrictions, these writers first sought personal satisfaction, and then addressed themselves to scholars rather than the people.

" 'But Hellenism found its medium in the Greek language, rich to satiety, and possessing a syntax of such extraordinary flexibility, that it could follow all evolutions without being shaken in its organism. It was in vain that the Latin literature sought to maintain its position by harking back to the writers anterior to Cicero, those that Hellenism had not touched, and presenting them as models of style; and thus a new school very fain of antiquity had sprung up, with Fronto for its acknowledged chief—a school pre-occupied above all things by the form; obsolete words set in a new setting, modern words introduced into old cadences to freshen them with a bright and delightful varnish, in a word, a language under visible sign of decay . . . yet how full of dim idea and evanescent music—a sort of Indian summer, a season of dependency that looked back on the splendours of Augustan yesterdays—an autumn forest.'

"Did you ever hear such rubbish, or affectation, whichever you like to call it? I should like to know what all that's to do with mediaeval Latin. And then he goes on to complain of the architecture of Stanton College. . . . It is, he says, base Tudor of the vilest kind. 'Practical cookery' he calls it, 'antique sauce, sold by all chemists and grocers.' Do you know what he means? I don't. And worst news of all, he is, would you believe it? putting a magnificent thirteen century window into the chapel, and he wants me to go up to London to make enquiries about organs. He is prepared to go as far as a thousand pounds. Did you ever hear of such a thing? Those Jesuits are encouraging-him. Of course it would just suit them if he became a priest; nothing would suit them better; the whole property would fall into their hands. Now, what I want you to do, my dear friend, is to go to Stanton College to-morrow, or next day, as soon as you possibly can, and to talk to John. You must tell him how unwise it is to spend fifteen hundred pounds in one year, building organs and putting up windows. His intentions are excellent, but his estate won't bear such extravagances: and everybody here thinks he is such a miser. I want you to tell him that he should marry. Just fancy what a terrible thing it would be if the estate passed away to distant relatives—to those terrible cousins of ours."

"Very well, Lizzie, I will do what I can. I will go to-morrow. I have not seen him for five years. The last time he was here I was away. I don't think it would be a bad notion to suggest that the Jesuits are after his money, that they are endeavouring to inveigle him into the priesthood in order that they may get hold of his property."

"No, no; you must not say such a thing. I will not have you say anything against his religion. I was very wrong to suggest such a thing. I am sure no such idea ever entered the Jesuits' heads. Perhaps I am wrong to send you to them. . . . . Now I depend on you not to speak to him on religious subjects."

CHAPTER II.

MRS NORTON had known William Hare all her life. She was the youngest daughter, he the youngest son of equal Yorkshire families. Separated by about a mile of pasture and woodland, these families had for generations lived unanimous lives. In England the hunting field, the grouse moor, the croquet and tennis lawn, with its charming adjunct the five-o'clock tea-table, have made life in certain classes almost communal; and Mrs Norton and William Hare had stood in white frocks under Christmas trees and shared sweetmeats. He often thought of the first time he saw her, wearing a skirt that fell below her ankles, with her hair done up. And she remembered his first appearance in evening clothes, and how surprised and delighted she was to hear him ask her if he might have the pleasure of a waltz.

He went to Oxford to take his degree; she was taken to London for the season, and towards the end of the third year she married Mr Norton, and went to live at Thornby Place. Through the excitement of the marriage arrangements, and the rapid impressions of her honeymoon, the thought of having for neighbour the playmate of her youth had flitted across, but had not rested in, her mind, and she did not realize the charm that it was for her until one afternoon, now more than twenty years ago, a young curate, bespattered with the grey mud of the downs, had startled her and her husband by addressing her as Lizzie. Lizzie she had remained to him, he was William to her, and henceforth their lives had been indissolubly linked. Not a week had passed without their seeing each other. There were visits to pay, there was hunting, and then habit intervened; and for many years, in suffering, in joy, in hope, their thoughts had instinctively looked to each other for reflective sympathy, and every remembrable event was full of mutual associations. He had sat by her when, after the birth of her first and only child, she lay pale, beautiful, and weak on a sofa by a window blown by the tide of summer scent; and the autumn of that same year he had walked with her in the garden, where the leaves fell like the last illusion of youth under the tears of an incurable grief; and staying in their walk they looked on the house which was to be for evermore one of widowhood.

Had she ever loved him? Had he ever loved her? In moments of passionate loneliness she had yearned for his protection; in moments of deep dejection he had dreamed of the happiness he might have found with her; but in the broad day of their lives they had ever thought of each other as friends. He had advised her on the management of her estate, on the education of her son; and in his afflictions—in his widowerhood—when his children quickly followed their mother to the grave, Mrs Norton's form, face, and words had steadied him, and had helped him to bear with a life of crumbling ruin. Kitty was now the only one that remained to him.

Mrs Norton had had projects of wealth and title for her son, but his continued disdain of women and the love of women had long since forced her to abandon her hopes, and now any one he might select she would gladly welcome; but she whom Mrs Norton would have preferred to all others was the daughter of her old friend. Her son had deserted her, and now all her affections were centred in Kitty. Kitty was as much at Thornby Place as at the Rectory, and in the gaiety of her bright eyes, and in the shine of her gold-brown hair—for ever slipping from the gold hair-pins in frizzed masses—Mrs Norton continued her dreams of her son's marriage.

Mr Hare thought it harsh that his daughter should be so constantly taken from him, but the parsonage was so lonely for Kitty, and there were luncheon and tennis parties at Thornby Place, and Mrs Norton took the girl out for drives, and together they visited all the county families. A suspicion of match-making sometimes crossed Mr Hare's mind, but it faded in the knowledge that John was always at Stanton College; and to send this fair flower to his great—to his only—friend, was a joy, and the bitterness of temporary loss was forgotten in the sweetness of the sharing. He had suffered much; but these last years had been quiet, free from despair at least, and he wished to drift a little longer with the tide of this time. Why strive to hasten events? If this thing was to be, it would be. So he had thought of his daughter's marriage. Fancies had long hung about the confines of his mind, but nothing had struck him with the full force of a thought until suddenly he understood the exact purport of his mission to Stanton College. He leaned forward as if he were going to tell the driver to return, but before he could do so the lodge-keeper opened the great gate, and the hansom cab rattled under the archway.

Then he viewed the scheme in general outline and in remote detail. It was very simple. Lizzie had been to Shoreham, and had taken Kitty away with her; he had been sent to Stanton College to beg John Norton to return to Thornby Place, and to say what he could in favour of marriage generally. This was very compromising. He had been deceived; Lizzie had deceived him. She had no right to do such a thing; and, striving to determine on a line of conduct, Mr Hare examined abstractedly the place he was passing through.

In large and serpentine curves the road wound through a wood of small beech trees—so small that in the November dishevelment the plantations were like so much brushwood; and, tying behind the wind-swept opening, gravel walks appeared in grey fragments, and the green spaces of the cricket field with a solitary divine reading his breviary. The drive turned and turned again in great sloping curves; more divines were passed, and then there came a long terrace with a balustrade and a view of the open country, now full of mist. And to see the sharp spire of the distant church you had to look closely, and slanting slowly upwards the great plain drew a long and melancholy line across the sky. The lower terrace was approached by an imposing flight of steps, there were myriads of leaves in the air, and the college bell rang in its high red tower.

The high red walls of the college faced the dismal terraces, and the triple line of diamond-paned and iron-barred windows stared upon the ugly Staffordshire landscape. A square tower squatted in the middle of the building, and out of it rose the octagon of the bell tower, and in the tower wall was the great oak door studded with great nails.

"How Birmingham the whole place does look," thought Mr Hare, as he laid his hand on an imitation mediaeval bell-pull.

"Is Mr John Norton at home?" he asked when the servant came. "Will you give him my card, and say that I should like to see him."

On entering, Mr Hare found himself in a tiled hall, around which was built a staircase in varnished oak. There was a quadrangle, and from three sides the interminable latticed windows looked down on the green sward; on the fourth there was an open corridor, with arches to imitate a cloister. All was strong and barren, and only about the varnished staircase was there any sign of comfort. There a virgin in bright blue stood on a crescent moon; above her the ceiling was panelled in oak, and the banisters, the cocoa nut matting, the bit of stained glass, and the religious prints, suggested a mock air of hieratic dignity. And the room Mr Hare was shown into continued this impression. Cabinets in carved oak harmonised with high-backed chairs glowing with red Utrecht velvet, and a massive table, on which lay a folio edition of St Augustine's "City of God" and the "Epistolæ Consolitoriæ" of St Jerome.

The bell continued to clang, and through the latticed windows Mr Hare watched the divines hurrying along the windy terrace, and the tramp of the boys going to their class-rooms could be heard in passages below.

Then a young man entered. He was thin, and he was dressed in black. His face was very Roman, the profile especially was what you might expect to find on a Roman coin—a high cheek-bone, a strong chin, and a large ear. The eyes were prominent and luminous, and the lower part of the face was expressive of resolution and intelligence, but above the eyes there were many indications of cerebral distortions. The forehead was broad, but the temples retreated rapidly to the brown hair which grew luxuriantly on the top of the head, leaving what the phrenologists call the bumps of ideality curiously exposed, and this, taken in conjunction with the yearning of the large prominent eyes, suggested at once a clear, delightful intelligence,—a mind timid, fearing, and doubting, such a one as would seek support in mysticism and dogma, that would rise instantly to a certain point, but to drop as suddenly as if sickened by the too intense light of the cold, pure heaven of reason to the gloom of the sanctuary and the consolations of Faith. Let us turn to the mouth for a further indication of character. It was large, the lips were thick, but without a trace of sensuality. They were dim in colour, they were undefined in shape, they were a little meaningless—no, not meaningless, for they confirmed the psychological revelations of the receding temples. The hands were large, powerful, and grasping; they were earthly hands; they were hands that could take and could hold, and their materialism was curiously opposed to the ideality of the eyes—an ideality that touched the confines of frenzy. The shoulders were square and carried well back, the head was round, with close-cut hair, the straight-falling coat was buttoned high, and the fashionable collar, with a black satin cravat, beautifully tied and relieved with a rich pearl pin, set another unexpected but singularly charmful detail to an aggregate of apparently irreconcilable characteristics.

"And how do you do, my dear Mr Hare? and who would have expected to see you here? I am so glad to see you."

These words were spoken frankly and cordially, and there was a note of mundane cheerfulness in the voice which did not quite correspond with the sacerdotal elegance of this young man. Then he added quickly, as if to save himself from asking the reason of this very unexpected visit—

"But you have never been here before; this is the first time you have seen our college. And seeing it as it now is, you would not believe all the delightful detail that a ray of sunlight awakens in that hideous brown monotony, soaked with rain and bedimmed with mist."

"Yes, I can quite understand that the college is not looking its best on a day like this. We have had very wet weather lately."

"No doubt, and I am afraid these late rains have interfered with the harvest. The accounts from the North are very alarming, but in Sussex, I suppose, everything was over at least two months ago. Still even there the farmers have been losing money for some time back. I have had to make some very heavy reductions. Pearson declared he could not possibly continue at the present rent with corn as low as eight pounds a load. This is very serious, but it is very difficult to arrive at the truth. I want to talk to you; but we shall have plenty of time presently; you'll stay and dine? And I'll show you over the college: you have never been here before, and now I come to reckon it up, I find I have not seen you for nearly five years."

"It must be very nearly that; I missed you the last time you were at Thornby Place, and that was three years ago."

"Three years! It sounds very shocking, doesn't it? to have a beautiful place in Sussex and not to live there: to prefer an ugly red-brick college—Birmingham Tudor; my mother invented the expression. When she is in a passion she hits on the very happiest concurrence of words; and I must say she is right,—the architecture here is appallingly ugly; and I don't think anything could be done to improve it, do you?"

"I can't say that I can suggest anything for the moment, but I thought it was for the sake of the architecture, which I frankly confess I don't in the least admire, that you lived here."

"You thought it was for the sake of the architecture. . . ."

"Then why do you not come home and spend Christmas with your mother!"

"Christmas! Well, I suppose I ought to. But it will be hard to bear with the plain Protestantism, the smug materialism of Sussex at such a season; and when one thinks what the day is commemorative of—"

"You surely do not mean that you would prefer to see the people starving? If your dislike of Protestantism rests only on roast beef and plum pudding. . ."

"No, you don't understand. But I beg your pardon—I had really forgotten. . ."

"Never mind," said Mr Hare smiling; "continue: we were talking of roast beef and plum pudding—"

"Well, roast beef and plum pudding, say what you like, is a very complete figuration of the Protestant ideal. Now let us think of Sussex. . . . The villas with their gables, and railings, and laurels, the snug farm-houses, the market-gardening, but especially the villas, so representative of a sleepy smug materialism. . . Oh, it is horrible; I cannot think of Sussex without a revulsion of feeling. Sussex is utterly opposed to the monastic spirit. Why, even the clowns are easy, yes, easy as one of the upholsterer's armchairs of the villa residences. And the aspect of the county tallies exactly with the state of soul of its people. In that southern county all is soft and lascivious; there is no wildness, none of that scenical grandeur which we find in Scotland and Ireland, and which is emblematic of the yearning of man's soul for something higher than this mean and temporal life."

There was rapture in John's eyes. With a quick movement of his hands he seemed to spurn the entire materialism of Sussex. After a pause, he continued:

"There is no asceticism in Sussex, there is no yearning for anything higher or better. You—yes, you and the whole place are, in every sense of the word. Conservative—that is to say, brutally satisfied with the present ordering of things."

"Now, now, my clear John, by your own account Pearson is not by any means so satisfied with the present condition of things as you yourself would wish him to be."

John laughed loudly, and it was clear that the paradox in no way displeased him.

"But we were speaking," he continued, "not of temporal, but of spiritual pains and penalties. Now, anyone who did not know me—and none will ever know me— would think that I had not a care in the world. Well, I have suffered as horribly, I have been tortured as cruelly, as ever poor mortal was. . . . I have lain on the floor of my room, my heart dead within me, and moaned and shrieked with horror."

"Horror of what?"

"Horror of death and a worse horror of life. Few amongst men ever realise the truth of things, but there are rare occasions, moments of supernatural understanding or suffering (which are two words for one and the same thing), when we see life in all its worm-like meanness, and death in its plain, stupid loathsomeness. Two days out of this year live like fire in my mind. I went to my uncle Richard's funeral. There was cold meat and sherry on the table; a dreadful servant asked me if I would go up to the corpse-room. (Mark the expression.) I went. It lay swollen and featureless, and two busy hags lifted it up and packed it tight with wisps of hay, and mechanically uttered shrieks and moans.

"But, though the funeral was painfully obscene, it was not so obscene as the view of life I was treated to last week. . . .

"Last week I was in London; I went to a place they call the 'Colonies.' Till then I had never realised the foulness of the human animal, but there even his foulness was overshadowed by his stupidity. The masses, yes, I saw the masses, and I fed with them in their huge intellectual stye. The air was filled with lines of the most inconceivable flags, lines upon lines of pale yellow, and there were glass cases filled with pickle bottles, and there were piles of ropes and a machine in motion, and in nooks there were some dreadful lay figures, and written underneath them, 'Indian corn-seller,' 'Indian fish-seller.' And there was the Prince of Wales on horseback, three times larger than life; and there were stuffed deer upon a rock, and a Polar bear, and the Marquis of Lorne underneath. In another room there were Indian houses, things in carved wood, and over each large placards announcing the popular dinner, the buffet, the table d'hôte, at half-a-crown; and there were oceans of tea, and thousands of rolls of butter, and in the gardens the band played 'Thine alone' and 'Mine again.'

"It seemed as if all the back-kitchens and staircases in England had that day been emptied out—life-tattered housewives, girls grown stout on porter, pretty-faced babies, heavy-handed fathers, whistling boys in their sloppy clothes, and attitudes curiously evidencing an odious domesticity. . . .

"In the Greek and Roman life there was an ideal, and there was a great ideal in the monastic life of the Middle Ages; but an ideal is wholly wanting in nineteenth century life. I am not of these later days. I am striving to come to terms with life."

"And you think you can do that best by folding vestments and reviling humanity. I do not see how you reconcile these opinions with the teaching of Christ—with the life of Christ."

"Oh, of course, if you are going to use those arguments against me, I have done; I can say no more."

Mr Hare did not answer, and at the end of a long silence John said:

"But, what do you say, supposing I show you over the college now, and when that's done you will come up to my room and we'll have a smoke before dinner?"

Mr Hare raised no objection, and the two men descended the staircase into the long stony corridor. The quadrangle filled the diamond panes of the latticed windows with green, and the divine walking to and fro was a spot of black. There were pictures along the walls of the corridor—pictures of upturned faces and clasped hands—and these drew words of commiseration for the artistic ignorance of the College authorities from John's lips.

"And they actually believe that that dreadful monk with the skull is a real Ribera. . . . The chapel is on the right, the refectory on the left. Come, let us see the chapel; I am anxious to hear what you think of my window."

"It ought to be very handsome; it cost five hundred, did it not?"

"No, not quite so much as that," John answered abruptly; and then, passing through the communion rails, they stood under the multi-coloured glory of three bishops. Mr Hare felt that a good deal of rapture was expected of him; but in his efforts to praise, he felt he was exposing his ignorance. John called attention to the transparency of the green-watered skies; and turning their backs on the bishops, the blue ceiling with the gold stars was declared, all things considered, to be in excellent taste. The benches in the body of the church were for boys; the carved chairs set along both walls between the communion rails and the first steps of the altar were for the divines. The president and vice-president knelt facing each other. The priests, deacons, and sub-deacons followed according to their rank. There were slenderer benches, and these were for the choir; and from a music-book placed on wings of the great golden eagle, the leader conducted the singing.

The side altar, with the rich Turkey carpet spread over the steps, was St George's, and further on, in an addition made lately, there were two more altars, dedicated respectively to the Virgin and St Joseph.

"The maid-servants kneel in that corner. I have often suggested that they should be moved out of sight. You do not understand me. Protestantism has always been more reconciled to the presence of women in sacred places than we. We would wish them beyond the precincts. And it is easy to imagine how the unspeakable feminality of those maid-servants jars a beautiful impression—the altar towering white with wax candles, the benedictive odour of incense, the richness of the vestments, treble voices of boys floating, and the sweetness of a long day spent about the sanctuary with flowers and chalices in my hands, fade in a sense of sullen disgust, in a revulsion of feeling which I will not attempt to justify."

Then his thoughts, straying back to sudden recollections of monastic usages and habits, he said:

"I should like to scourge them out of this place." And then, half playfully, half seriously, and wholly conscious of the grotesqueness, he added:

"Yes, I am not at all sure that a good whipping would not do them good. They should be well whipped. I believe that there is much to be said in favour of whipping."

Mr Hare did not answer. He listened like one in a dark and unknown place. But, as if unconscious of the embarrassment he was creating, John told of the number of masses that were said daily, and of the eagerness shown by the boys to obtain an altar. Altar service was rewarded by a large piece of toast for breakfast. Handsome lads of sixteen were chosen for acolytes, the torch-bearers were selected from the smallest boys, the office of censer was filled by John Norton, and he was also the chief sacristan, and had charge of the altar plate and linen and the vestments. He spoke of the organ, and he depreciated the present instrument, and enlarged upon some technical details anent the latest modern improvements in keys and stops.

They went up to the organ loft. John would play his setting of St Ambrose's hymn, "Veni redemptor gentium," if Mr Hare would go to the bellows, and feeling as if he were being turned into ridicule, Mr Hare took his place at the handle; and he found it even more embarrassing to give an opinion on the religiosity of the music, than on the archaeological colouration of the bishops in the window. But John did not court any very detailed criticism on his hymn, and alluding to the fact that even in the fourth century accent was beginning to replace quantity, he led the way to the sacristy.

And it was impossible to avoid noticing that the opening of the carved oaken presses, smelling sweet and benignly of orris root and lavender, acted on John almost as a physical pleasure, and also that his hands seemed nervous with delight as he unfolded the jewelled embroideries, and smoothed out the fine linen of the under vestments; and his voice, too, seemed to gain a sharp tenderness and emotive force, as he told how these were the gold vestments worn by the bishop, and only on certain great feast-days, and that these were the white vestments worn on days especially commemorative of the Virgin. The consideration of the censers, candlesticks, chalices, and albs took some time, and John was a little aggressive in his explanation of Catholic ceremonial, and its grace and comeliness compared with the stiffness and materialism of the Protestant service.

From the sacristy they went to the boys' library. John pointed out the excellent supply of light literature that the bookcases contained.

"We take travels, history, fairy-tales—romances of all kinds, so long as sensual passion is not touched upon at any length. Of course we don't object to a book in which just towards the end the young man falls in love and proposes; but there must not be much of that sort of thing. Here are Robert Louis Stevenson's works, 'Treasure Island,' 'Kidnapped' &c, charming writer—a neat pretty style, with a pleasant souvenir of Edgar Poe running through it all. You have no idea how the boys enjoy his books."

"And don't you?"

"Oh no; I have just glanced at him: for my own reading, I can admit none who does not write in the first instance for scholars, and then to the scholarly instincts in readers generally. Here is Walter Pater. We have his Renaissance; studies in art and poetry—I gave it myself to the library. We were so sorry we could not include that most beautiful book, "Marius the Epicurean." We have some young men here of twenty and three and twenty, and it would be delightful to see them reading it, so exquisite is its hopeful idealism; but we were obliged to bar it on account of the story of Psyche, sweetly though it be told, and sweetly though it be removed from any taint of realistic suggestion. Do you know the book?"

"I can't say I do."

"Then read it at once. It is a breath of delicious fragrance blown back to us from the antique world; nothing is lost or faded, the bloom of that glad bright world is upon every page; the wide temples, the lustral water—the youths apportioned out for divine service, and already happy with a sense of dedication, the altars gay with garlands of wool and the more sumptuous sort of flowers, the colour of the open air, with the scent of the beanfields, mingling with the cloud of incense."

"But I thought you denied any value to the external world, that the spirit alone was worth considering."

"The antique world knew how to idealise, and if they delighted in the outward form, they did not leave it gross and vile as we do when we touch it; they raised it, they invested it with a sense of aloofness that we know not of. Flesh or spirit, idealise one or both, and I will accept them. But you do not know the book. You must read it. Never did I read with such rapture of being, of growing to spiritual birth. It seemed to me that for the first time I was made known to myself; for the first time the false veil of my grosser nature was withdrawn, and I looked into the true ethereal eyes, pale as wan water and sunset skies, of my higher self. Marius was to me an awakening; the rapture of knowledge came upon me that even our temporal life might be beautiful; that, in a word, it was possible to somehow come to terms with life. . . . You must read it. For instance, can anyone conceive anything more perfectly beautiful than the death of Flavian, and all that youthful companionship, and Marius' admiration for his friend's poetry? . . . . that delightful language of the third century—a new Latin, a season of dependency, an Indian summer full of strange and varied cadences, so different from the monotonous sing-song of the Augustan age; the school of which Fronto was the head. Indeed, it was Pater's book that first suggested to me the idea of the book I am writing. But perhaps you do not know I am writing a book. . . . Did my mother tell you anything about it?"

"Yes; she told me you were writing the history of Christian Latin."

"Yes; that is to say, of the language that was the literary, the scientific, and the theological language of Europe for more than a thousand years."

And talking of his book rapidly, and with much boyish enthusiasm, John opened the doors of the refectory. The long, oaken tables, the great fireplace, and the stained glass seemed to delight him, and he alluded to the art classes of monastic life. The class-rooms were peeped into, the playground was viewed through the lattice windows, and they went to John's room, up a staircase curiously carpeted with lead.

John's rooms! a wide, bright space of green painted wood and straw matting. The walls were panelled from floor to ceiling. In the centre of the floor there was an oak table—a table made of sharp slabs of oak laid upon a frame that was evidently of ancient design, probably early German, a great, gold screen sheltered a high canonical chair with elaborate carvings, and on a reading-stand close by lay the manuscript of a Latin poem.

"And what is this?" said Mr Hare.

"Oh I that is a poem by Milo, his 'De Sobricate.' I heard that the manuscript was still preserved in the convent of Saint Amand, near Tournai, and I sent and had a copy made for me. That was the simplest way. You have no idea how difficult it is to buy the works of any Latin authors except those of the Augustan age. Milo was a monk, and he lived in the eighth century. He was a man of very considerable attainments, if he were not a very great poet. He was a contemporary of Florus, who, by the way, was a real poet. Some of his verses are delightful, full of delicate cadence and colour. The MS. under your hand is a poem by him—

'Montes et colles, silvseque et flumina, fontes, Præmptseque rapes, pariter vallesque profondæ Francorum lugete genus: quod mimere christi, Imperio celsum jacet ecce in pulvere mersum.'

That was written in the eighth century when the language was becoming terribly corrupt; when it was hideous with popular idiom barbarously and recklessly employed. But even in that time of autumnal decay and pallid bloom, a real poet such as Walahfrid Strabat could weave a garland of grace and beauty; one, indeed, that lived through the chance of centuries in the minds of men. It found numberless imitators and favour even with the Humanists, and it was reprinted eight times in the seventeenth century. This poem is of especial interest to me on account of the illustration it affords of a theory of my own concerning the unconsciousness of the true artist. For breaking away from the literary habitudes of his time, which were to do the gospels or the life of a favourite saint into hexameters, he wrote a poem, 'Hortulus' descriptive of the garden of the monastery. The garden was all the world to the monks; it furnished them at once with the pleasures and the necessaries of their lives. Walahfrid felt this; he described his feelings, and he produced a chef d'œuvre." Going over to the bookcase, John took down a volume. He read:—

"'Hoc nemus umbriferum pingit viridissima Kutæ Silvula cæruleæ, foliis quæ prædita parvis, Umbellas jaculata brevis, spiramina venti Et radios Phœbi caules transmittit ad imos, Attactuque graves leni dispergit odores, Hæc cum multiplici vigeat virtute raedelæ, Dicitur occultis apprime obstare venenis, Toxicaque invasis incommoda pellere fibris.'

Now, can anything be more charming? True it is that pingit in the first line does not seem to construe satisfactorily, and I am not certain that the poet may not have written *fingit.* Fingit would not be pure Latin, but that is beside the question."

"Indeed it is. I must say I prefer the Georgics. I have known many strange tastes, but your fancy for bad Latin is the strangest of all."

"Classical Latin, with the exception of Tacitus, is cold-blooded and self-satisfied. There is no agitation, no fever; to me it is utterly without interest."

To the books and manuscripts the pictures on the walls afforded an abrupt contrast. No. 1. "A Japanese Girl," by Monet. A poppy in the pale green walls; a wonderful macaw! Why does it not speak in strange dialect? It trails lengths of red silk. Such red! The pigment is twirled and heaped with quaint device, until it seems to be beautiful embroidery rather than painting; and the straw-coloured hair, and the blond light on the face, and the unimaginable coquetting of that fan. . . .

No. 2. "The Drop Curtain," by Degas. The drop curtain is fast descending; only a yard of space remains. What a yardful of curious comment, what satirical note on the preposterousness of human existence! what life there is in every line; and the painter has made meaning with every blot of colour! Look at the two principal dancers! They are down on their knees, arms raised, bosoms advanced, skirts extended, a hundred coryphées are clustered about them. Leaning hands, uplifted necks, painted eyes, scarlet mouths, a piece of thigh, arched insteps, and all is blurred; vanity, animalism, indecency, absurdity, and all to be whelmed into oblivion in a moment. Wonderful life; wonderful Degas!

No. 3. "A Suburb," by Monet. Snow! the world is white. The furry fluff has ceased to fall, and the sky is darkling and the night advances, dragging the horizon up with it like a heavy, deadly curtain. But the roof of the villa is white, and the green of the laurels shaken free of the snow shines through the railings, and the shadows that lie across the road leading to town are blue—yes, as blue as the slates under the immaculate snow.

No. 4. "The Cliff's Edge," by Monet. Blue? purple the sea is; no, it is violet; 'tis striped with violet and flooded with purple; there are living greens, it is full of fading blues. The dazzling sky deepens as it rises to breathless azure, and the soul pines for and is fain of God. White sails show aloft; a line of dissolving horizon; a fragment of overhanging cliff wild with coarse grass and bright with poppies, and musical with the lapsing of the summer waves.

There were in all six pictures—a tall glass filled with pale roses, by Renoir; a girl tying up her garter, by Monet.

Through the bedroom door Mr Hare saw a narrow iron bed, an iron washhand-stand, and a priedieu. A curious three-cornered wardrobe stood in one corner, and facing it, in front of the priedieu, a life-size Christ hung with outstretched arms. The parson looked round for a seat, but the chairs were like cottage stools on high legs, and the angular backs looked terribly knife-like.

"Sit in the arm-chair. Shall I get you a pillow from the next room? Personally I cannot bear upholstery; I cannot conceive anything more hideous than a padded arm-chair. All design is lost in that infamous stuffing. Stuffing is a vicious excuse for the absence of design. If upholstery was forbidden by law to-morrow, in ten years we should have a school of design. Then the necessity of composition would be imperative.

"I daresay there is a good deal in what you say; but tell me, don't you find these chairs very uncomfortable. Don't you think that you would find a good comfortable arm-chair very useful for reading purposes?"

"No, I should feel far more uncomfortable on a cushion than I do on this bit of hard oak. Our ancestors had an innate sense of form that we have not. Look at these chairs, nothing can be plainer; a cottage stool is hardly more simple, and yet they are not offensive to the eye. I had them made from a picture by Albert Durer. But tell me, what will you take to drink? Will you have a glass of champagne, or a brandy and soda, or what do you say to an absinthe?"

"'Pon my word, you seem to look after yourself. You don't forget the inner man."

"I always keep a good supply of liquor; have a cigar?" And John passed to him a box of fragrant and richly coloured Havanas. . . . Mr Hare took a cigar, and glanced at the table on which John was mixing the drinks. It was a slip of marble, rested, cafe fashion, on iron supports.

"But that table is modern, surely?—quite modern!"

"Quite; it is a café table, but it does not offend my eye. You surely would not have me collect a lot of old-fashioned furniture and pile it up in my rooms, Turkey carpets and Japaneseries of all sorts; a room such as Sir Fred. Leighton would declare was intended to be merely beautiful."

Striving vainly to understand, Mr Hare drank his brandy and soda in silence. Presently he walked over to the bookcases. There were two: one was filled with learned-looking volumes bearing the names of Latin authors; and the parson, who prided himself on his Latinity, was surprised, and a little nettled, to find so much ignorance proved upon him. With Tertullian, St Jerome, and St Augustine he was of course acquainted, but of Lactantius, Prudentius, Sedulius, St Fortunatus, Duns Scotus, Hibernicus exul, Angilbert, Milo, &c., he was obliged to admit he knew nothing—even the names were unknown to him.

In the bookcase on the opposite side of the room there were complete editions of Landor and Swift, then came two large volumes on Leonardo da Vinci. Raising his eyes, the parson read through the titles of Mr Browning's work. Tennyson was in a cheap seven-and-six edition; then came Swinburne, Pater, Rossetti, Morris, two novels by Rhoda Broughton, Dickens, Thackeray, Fielding, and Smollett; the complete works of Balzac, Gautier's Emaux et Camées, Salammbo, L'Assommoir; add to this Carlyle, Byron, Shelley, Keats, &c.

At the end of a long silence, Mr Hare said, glancing once again at the Latin authors, and walking towards the fire:

"Tell me, John, are those the books you are writing about? Supposing you explain to me in a few words the line you are taking. Your mother tells me that you intend to call your book the History of Christian Latin."

"Yes, I had thought of using that title, but I am afraid it is a little too ambitious. To write the history of a literature extending over at least eight centuries would entail an appalling amount of reading; and besides only a few, say a couple of dozen writers out of some hundreds, are of the slightest literary interest, and very few indeed of any real aesthetic value. I have been hard at work lately, and I think I know enough of the literature of the Middle Ages to enable me to make a selection that will comprise everything of interest to ordinary scholarship, and enough to form a sound basis to rest my own literary theories upon. I begin by stating that there existed in the Middle Ages a universal language such as Goethe predicted the future would again bring to us. . . .

"Before the formation of the limbs, that is to say before the German and Roman languages were developed up to the point of literary usage, the Latin language was the language of all nations of the western world. But the day came, in some countries a little earlier, in some a little later, when it was replaced by the national idioms. The different literatures of the West had therefore been preceded by a Latin literature that had for a long time held out a supporting hand to each. The language of this literature was not a dead language, It was the language of government, of science, of religion; and a little dislocated, a little barbarised, it had penetrated to the minds of the people, and found expression in drinking songs and street ditties.

"Such is the theme of my book; and it seems to me that a language that has played so important a part in the world's history is well worthy of serious study.

"I show how Christianity, coming as it did with a new philosophy, and a new motive for life, invigorated and saved the Latin language in a time of decline and decrepitude. For centuries it had given expression, even to satiety, to a naive joy in the present; on this theme, all that could be said had been said, all that could be sung had been sung, and the Rhetoricians were at work with alliteration and refrain when Christianity came, and impetuously forced the language to speak the desire of the soul. In a word, I want to trace the effect that such a radical alteration in the music, if I may so speak, had upon the instrument—the Latin language."

"And with whom do you begin?" "With Tertullian, of course." "And what do you think of him?"

"Tertullian, one of the most fascinating characters of ancient or modern times. In my study of his writings I have worked out a psychological study of the man himself as revealed through them. His realism, I might say materialism, is entirely foreign to my own nature, but I cannot help being attracted by that wild African spirit, so full of savage contradictions, so full of energy that it never knew repose: in him you find all the imperialism of ancient times. When you consider that he lived in a time when the church was struggling for utterance amid the horrors of persecution, his mad Christianity becomes singularly attractive; a passionate fear of beauty for reason of its temptations, a fear that turned to hatred, and forced him at last into the belief that Christ was an ugly man."

"I know nothing of the monks of the eighth century and their poetry, but I do know something of Tertullian, and you mean to tell me that you admire his style—those harsh chopped-up phrases and strained antitheses."

"I should think I did. Phrases set boldly one against the other; quaint, curious, and full of colour, the reader supplies with delight the connecting link, though the passion and the force of the description lives and reels along. Listen:

"'Quæ tune spectaculi latitudo! quid admirer? quid rideam? ubi gaudeam? ubi exultem, spectans tot ac tantos reges, qui in cœlum recepti nuntiabantur, cum ipso Jove et ipsis suis testibus in imis tenebris congemiscentes!—Tunc magis tragædi audiendi, magis scilicet vocales in sua propria calamitate; tunc histriones cognoscendi, solutiores multo per ignem; tunc spectandus auriga, in flammea rota totus rubens, &c.'

"Show me a passage in Livy equal to that for sheer force and glittering colour. The phrases are not all dove-tailed one into the other and smoothed away; they stand out."

"Indeed they do. And whom do you speak of next?"

"I pass on to St Cyprian and Lactantius; to the latter I attribute the beautiful poem of the Phœnix."

"What! Claudian's poem?"

"No, but one infinitely superior. After Lactantius comes St Ambrose, St Jerome, and St Augustine. The second does not interest me, and my notice of him is brief; but I make special studies of the first and last. It was St Ambrose who introduced singing into the Catholic service. He took the idea from the Arians. He saw the effect it had upon the vulgar mind, and he resolved to combat the heresy with its own weapons. He composed a vast number of hymns. Only four have come down to us, and they are as perfect in form as in matter. You will scarcely find anywhere a false quantity or a hiatus. The Ambrosian hymns remained the type of all the hymnic poetry of succeeding centuries. Even Prudentius, great poet as he was, was manifestly influenced in the choice of metre and the composition of the strophe by the Deus Creator omnium. . . .

"St Ambrose did more than any other writer of his time to establish certain latent tendencies as characteristics of the Catholic spirit. His pleading in favour of ascetic life and of virginity, that entirely Christian virtue, was very influential. He lauds the virgin above the wife, and, indeed, he goes so far as to tell parents that they can obtain pardon of their sins by offering their daughters to God. His teaching in this respect was productive of very serious rebellion against what some are pleased to term the laws of Nature. But St Ambrose did not hesitate to uphold the repugnance of girls to marriage as not only lawful but praiseworthy."

"I am afraid you let your thoughts dwell very much on such subjects."

"Really, do you think I do?" John's eyes brightened for a moment, and he lapsed into what seemed an examination of conscience. Then he said, somewhat abruptly, "St Jerome I speak of, or rather I allude to him, and pass on at once to the study of St Augustine—the great prose writer, as Prudentius was the great poet, of the Middle Ages.

"Now, talking of style, I will admit that the eternal apostrophising of God and the incessant quoting from the New Testament is tiresome to the last degree, and seriously prejudices the value of the 'Confessions' as considered from the artistic standpoint. But when he bemoans the loss of the friend of his youth, when he tells of his resolution to embrace an ascetic life, he is nervously animated, and is as psychologically dramatic as Balzac.

"I have taken great pains with my study of St Augustine, because in him the special genius of Christianity for the first time found a voice. All that had gone before was a scanty flowerage—he was the perfect fruit. I am speaking from a purely artistic standpoint: all that could be done for the life of the senses had been clone, but heretofore the life of the soul had been lived in silence—none had come to speak of its suffering, its uses, its tribulation. In the time of Horace it was enough to sit in Lalage's bower and weave roses; of the communion of souls none had ever thought. Let us speak of the soul! This is the great dividing line between the pagan and Christian world, and St Augustine is the great landmark. In literature he discovered that man had a soul, and that man had grown interested in its story, had grown tired of the exquisite externality of the nymph-haunted forest and the waves where the Triton blows his plaintive blast.

"The whole theory and practice of modern literature is found in the 'Confessions of St Augustine;' and from hence flows the great current of psychological analysis which, with the development of the modern novel, grows daily greater in volume and more penetrating in essence. . . . Is not the fretful desire of the Balzac novel to tell of the soul's anguish an obvious development of the 'Confessions'?

"In like manner I trace the origin of the ballad, most particularly the English ballad, to Prudentius, a contemporary of Claudian."

"You don't mean to say that you trace back our north-country ballads to, what do you call him?"

"Prudentius. I show that there is much in his hymns that recalls the English ballads."

"In his hymns?"

"Yes; in the poems that come under such denomination. I confess it is not a little puzzling to find a narrative poem of some five hundred lines or more included under the heading of hymns; it would seem that nearly all lyric poetry of an essentially Christian character was so designated, to separate it from secular or pagan poetry. In Prudentins' first published work, 'Liber Cathemerinon,' we find hymns composed absolutely after the manner of St Ambrose, in the same or in similar metres, but with this difference, the hymns of Prudentius are three, four, and sometimes seven times longer than those of St Ambrose. The Spanish poet did not consider, or he lost sight of, the practical usages of poetry. He sang more from an artistic than a religious impulse. That he delighted in the song for the song's own sake is manifest; and this is shown in the variety of his treatment, and the delicate sense of music which determined his choice of metre. His descriptive writing is full of picturesque expression. The fifth hymn, 'Ad Incensum Lucernæ,' is glorious with passionate colour and felicitous cadence, be he describing with precious solicitude for Christian archæology the different means of artistic lighting, flambeaux, candles, lamps, or dreaming with all the rapture of a southern dream of the balmy garden of Paradise.

"But his best book to my thinking is by far, 'Peristephanon,' that is to say, the hymns celebrating the glory of the martyrs.

"I was saying just now that the hymns of Prudentius, by the dramatic rapidity of the narrative, by the composition of the strophe, and by their wit, remind me very forcibly of our English ballads. Let us take the story of St Laurence, written in iambics, in verses of four lines each. In the time of the persecutions of Valerian, the Roman prefect, devoured by greed, summoned St Laurence, the treasurer of the church, before him, and on the plea that parents were making away with their fortunes to the detriment of their children, demanded that the sacred vessels should be given up to him. 'Upon all coins is found the head of the Emperor and not that of Christ, therefore obey the order of the latter, and give to the Emperor what belongs to the Emperor.'

"To this speech, peppered with irony and sarcasm, St Laurence replies that the church is very rich, even richer than the Emperor, and that he will have much pleasure in offering its wealth to the prefect, and he asks for three days to classify the treasures. Transported with joy, the prefect grants the required delay. Laurence collects the infirm who have been receiving charity from the church; and in picturesque grouping the poet shows us the blind, the paralytic, the lame, the lepers, advancing with trembling and hesitating steps. Those are the treasures, the golden vases and so forth, that the saint has catalogued and is going to exhibit to the prefect, who is waiting in the sanctuary. The prefect is dumb with rage; the saint observes that gold is found in dross; that the disease of the body is to be less feared than that of the soul; and he develops this idea with a good deal of wit. The boasters suffer from dropsy, the miser from cramp in the wrist, the ambitious from febrile heat, the gossipers, who delight in tale-bearing, from the itch; but you, he says, addressing the prefect, you who govern Rome, [Footnote *: Qui Romam regis.] suffer from the *morbus regius* (you see the pun). In revenge for thus slighting his dignity, the prefect condemns St Laurence to be roasted on a slow fire, adding, 'and deny there, if you will, the existence of my Vulcan.' Even on the gridiron Laurence does not lose his good humour, and he gets himself turned as a cook would a chop.

"Now, do you not understand what I mean when I say that the hymns of Prudentius are an anticipation of the form of the English ballad? . . . . And in the fifth hymn the story of St Vincent is given with that peculiar dramatic terseness that you find nowhere except in the English ballad. But the most beautiful poem of all is certainly the fourteenth and last hymn. In a hundred and thirty-three hendecasyllabic verses the story of a young virgin condemned to a house of ill-fame is sung with exquisite sense of grace and melody. She is exposed naked at the corner of a street. The crowd piously turns away; only one young man looks upon her with lust in his heart. He is instantly struck blind by lightning, but at the request of the virgin his sight is restored to him. Then follows the account of how she suffered martyrdom by the sword—a martyrdom which the girl salutes with a transport of joy. The poet describes her ascending to Heaven, and casting one last look upon this miserable earth, whose miseries seem without end, and whose joys are of such short duration.

"Then his great poem 'Psychomachia' is the first example in mediaeval literature of allegorical poetry, the most Christian of all forms of art.

"Faith, her shoulders bare, her hair free, advances, eager for the fight. The 'cult of the ancient gods,' with forehead chapleted after the fashion of the pagan priests, dares to attack her, and is overthrown. The legion of martyrs that Faith has called together cry in triumphant unison. . . . . Modesty (Pudicitia), a young virgin with brilliant arms, is attacked by 'the most horrible of the Furies' (Sodomita Libido), who, with a torch burning with pitch and sulphur, seeks to strike her eyes, but Modesty disarms him and pierces him with her sword. 'Since the Virgin without stain gave birth to the Man-God, Lust is without rights in the world.' Patience watches the fight; she is presently attacked by Anger, first with violent words, and then with darts, which fall harmlessly from her armour. Accompanied by Job, Patience retires triumphant. But at that moment, mounted on a wild and unbridled steed, and covered with a lionskin, Pride (Superbia), her hair built up like a tower, menaces Humility (Mens humilis). Under the banner of Humility are ranged Justice, Frugality, Modesty, pale of face, and likewise Simplicity. Pride mocks at this miserable army, and would crush it under the feet of her steed. But she falls in a ditch dug by Fraud. Humility hesitates to take advantage of her victory; but Hope draws her sword, cuts off the head of the enemy, and flies away on golden wings to Heaven.

"Then Lust (Luxuria), the new enemy, appears. She comes from the extreme East, this wild dancer, with odorous hair, provocative glance and effeminate voice; she stands in a magnificent chariot drawn by four horses; she scatters violet and rose leaves; they are her weapons; their insidious perfumes destroy courage and will, and the army, headed by the virtues, speaks of surrender. But suddenly Sobriety (Sobrietas) lifts the standard of the Cross towards the sky. Lust falls from her chariot, and Sobriety fells her with a stone. Then all her saturnalian army is scattered. Love casts away his quiver. Pomp strips herself of her garments, and Voluptuousness (Voluptas) fears not to tread upon thorns, &c. But Avarice disguises herself in the mask of

Economy, and succeeds in deceiving all hearts until she is overthrown finally by Mercy (Operatica). All sorts of things happen, but eventually the poem winds up with a prayer to Christ, in which we learn that the soul shall fall again and again in the battle, and that this shall continue until the coming of Christ."

"'Tis very curious, very curious indeed. I know nothing of this literature."

"Very few do."

"And you have, I suppose, translated some of these poems?"

"I give a complete translation of the second hymn, the story of St Laurence, and I give long extracts from the poem we have been speaking about, and likewise from 'Hamartigenia,' which, by the way, some consider as his greatest work. And I show more completely, I think, than any other commentator, the analogy between it and the 'Divine Comedy,' and how much Dante owed to it. . . . Then the 'terza rima' was undoubtedly borrowed from the fourth hymn of the 'Cathemerinon.' ". . .

"You said, I think, that Prudentius was a contemporary of Claudian. Which do you think the greater poet?"

"Prudentius by far. Claudian's Latin was no doubt purer and his verse was better, that is to say, from the classical standpoint it was more correct."

"Is there any other standpoint?"

"Of course. There is pagan Latin and Christian Latin: Burns' poems are beautiful, and they are not written in Southern English; Chaucer's verse is exquisitely melodious, although it will not scan to modern pronunciation. In the earliest Christian poetry there is a tendency to write by accent rather than by quantity, but that does not say that the hymns have not a quaint Gothic music of their own. This is very noticeable in Sedulius, a poet of the fifth century. His hymn to Christ is not only full of assonance, but of all kinds of rhyme and even double rhymes. We find the same thing in Sedonius, and likewise in Fortunatus—a gay prelate, the morality of whose life is, I am afraid, open to doubt. . . .

"He had all the qualities of a great poet, but he wasted his genius writing love verses to Radegonde. The story is a curious one. Radegonde was the daughter of the King of Thuringia; she was made prisoner by Clotaire I., son of Clovis, who forced her to become his wife. On the murder of her father by her husband, she fled and founded a convent at Poictiers. There she met Fortunatus, who, it appears, loved her. It is of course humanly possible that their love was not a guilty one, but it is certain that the poet wasted the greater part of his life writing verses to her and her adopted daughter Agnes. In a beautiful poem in praise of virginity, composed in honour of Agnes, he speaks in a very disgusting way of the love with which nuns regard our Redeemer, and the recompence that awaits them in Heaven for their chastity. If it had not been for the great interest attaching to his verse as an example of the radical alteration that had been effected in the language, I do not think I should have spoken of this poet. Up to his time rhyme had slipped only occasionally into the verse, it had been noticed and had been allowed to remain by poets too idle to remove it, a strange something not quite understood, and yet not a wholly unwelcome intruder; but in St Fortunatus we find for the first time rhyme cognate with, the metre, and used with certainty and brilliancy. In the opening lines of the hymn, 'Vexilla Regis,' rhyme is used with superb effect. . . .

"But for signs of the approaching dissolution of the language, of its absorption by the national idiom, we must turn to St Gregory of Tours. He was a man of defective education, and the ***lingua rustica*** of France as it was spoken by the people makes itself felt throughout his writings. His use of ***iscere*** for ***escere,*** of the accusative for the ablative, one of St Gregory's favourite forms of speech, ***pro or quod*** for ***quoniam,*** conformable to old French ***porceque,*** so common for ***parceque.*** And while national idiom was oozing through grammatical construction, national forms of verse were replacing the classical metres which, so far as syllables were concerned, had hitherto been adhered to. As we advance into the sixth and seventh centuries, we find English monks attempting to reproduce the characteristics of Anglo-Saxon alliterative verse in Latin; and at the Court of Charlemagne we find an Irish monk writing Latin verse in a long trochaic line, which is native in Irish poetry.

"Poets were plentiful at the court of Charlemagne. Now, Angilbert was a poet of exquisite grace, and surprisingly modern is his music, which is indeed a wonderful anticipation of the lilt of Edgar Poe. I compare it to Poe. Just listen:—

"'Surge meo Domno clulces fac, fistula versus: David amat versus, surge et fac fistula versus. David amat vates, vatorum est gloria David Qua propter vates cuncti coucurrite in unum Atque meo David dulces cantate camœnas. David amat vates, vatorum est gloria David. Dulcis amor David inspirat corda canentum, Cordibus in nostris faciat amor ipsius odas: Vates Homerus amat David, fac, fistula, versus. David amat vates, vatorum est gloria David.' "

"I should have flogged that monk—'ipsius,' oh, oh!—'vatorum.' . . . It really is too terrible."

John laughed, and was about to reply, when the clanging of the college bell was heard.

"I am afraid that is dinner-time."

"Afraid, I am delighted; you don't suppose that every one can live, chameleon-like, on air, or worse still, on false quantities. Ha, ha, ha! And those pictures too. That snow is more violet than white."

When dinner was over, John and Mr Hare walked out on the terrace. The carriage waited in the wet in front of the great oak portal; the grey, stormy evening descended on the high roofs, smearing the red out of the walls and buttresses, and melancholy and tall the red college seemed amid its dwarf plantation, now filled with night wind and drifting leaves. Shadow and mist had floated out of the shallows above the crests of the valley, and the lamps of the farm-houses gleamed into a pale existence.

"And now tell me what I am to say to your mother. Will you come home for Christmas?"

"I suppose I must. I suppose it would seem so unkind if I didn't. I cannot account even to myself for my dislike to the place. I cannot think of it without a revulsion of feeling that is strangely personal."

"I won't argue that point with you, but I think you ought to come home."

"Why? Why ought I to come to Sussex, and marry my neighbour's daughter?"

"There is no reason that you should marry your neighbour's daughter, but I take it that you do not propose to pass your life here."

"For the present I am concerned mainly with the problem of how I may make advances, how I may meet life, as it were, half-way; for if possible I would not quite lose touch of the world. I would love to live in its shadow, a spectator whose duty it is to watch and encourage, and pity the hurrying throng on the stage. The church would approve this attitude, whereas hate and loathing of humanity are not to be justified. But I can do nothing to hurry the state of feeling I desire, except of course to pray. I have passed through some terrible moments of despair and gloom, but these are now wearing themselves away, and I am feeling more at rest."

Then, as if from a sudden fear of ridicule, John said, laughing: "Besides, looking at the question from a purely practical side, it must be hardly wise for me to return to society for the present. I like neither fox-hunting, marriage, Robert Louis Stevenson's stories, nor Sir Frederick Leighton's pictures; I prefer monkish Latin to Virgil, and I adore Degas, Monet, Manet, and Renoir, and since this is so, and alas, I am afraid irrevocably so, do you not think that I should do well to keep outside a world in which I should be the only wrong and vicious being? Why spoil that charming thing called society by my unlovely presence?

"Selfishness! I know what you are going to say—here is my answer. I assure you I administer to the best of my ability the fortune God gave me—I spare myself no trouble. I know the financial position of every farmer on my estate, the property does not owe fifty pounds;—I keep the tenants up to the mark; I do not approve of waste and idleness, but when a little help is wanted I am ready to give it. And then, well, I don't mind telling you, but it must not go any further. I have made a will leaving something to all my tenants; I give away a fixed amount in charity yearly."

"I know, my dear John, I know your life is not a dissolute one; but your mother is very anxious, remember you are the last. Is there no chance of your ever marrying?"

"I don't think I could live with a woman; there is something very degrading, something very gross in such relations. There is a better and a purer life to lead . . . an inner life, coloured and permeated with feelings and tones that are, oh, how intensely our own, and he who may have this life, shrinks from any adventitious presence that might jar or destroy it. To keep oneself unspotted, to feel conscious of no sense of stain, to know, yes, to hear the heart repeat that this self—hands, face, mouth and skin—is free from all befouling touch, is all one's own. I have always been strongly attracted to the colour white, and I can so well and so acutely understand the legend that tells that the ermine dies of gentle loathing of its own self, should a stain come upon its immaculate fur . . . . I should not say a legend, for that implies that the story is untrue, and it is not untrue—so beautiful a thought could not be untrue."

CHAPTER III.

"URNS on corner walls, pilasters, circular windows, flowerage and loggia. What horrible taste, and quite out of keeping with the landscape!" He rang the bell.

"How do you do, Master John!" cried the tottering old butler who had known him since babyhood. "Very glad, indeed, we all are to see you home again, sir!"

Neither the appellation of Master John, nor the sight of the four paintings, Spring, Summer, Autumn, and Winter, which decorated the walls of the passage, found favour with John, and the effusiveness of Mrs Norton, who rushed out of the drawing-room, followed by Kitty, and embraced her son, at once set on edge all his curious antipathies. Why this kissing, this approachment of flesh? Of course she was his mother. . . . Then this smiling girl in the background! He would have to amuse her and talk to her; what infinite boredom it would be! He trusted fervently that her visit would not be a long one.

Then through what seemed to him the pollution of triumph, he was led into the library; and he noticed, notwithstanding the presiding busts of Shakespeare and Milton, that there was but one wretched stand full of books in the room, and that in the gloom of a far corner. His mother sat down, and there was a resoluteness in her look and attitude that seemed to proclaim, "Now I hold you captive; "but she said:

"I was very much alarmed, my dear John, about your not sleeping. Mr Hare told me you said that you went two and three nights without closing your eyes, and that you had to have recourse to sleeping draughts."

"Not at all, mother, I never took a sleeping draught but twice in my life."

"Well, you don't sleep well, and I am sure it is those college beds. But you will be far more comfortable here. You are in the best bedroom in the house, the one in front of the staircase, the bridal chamber; and I have selected the largest and softest feather-bed in the house."

"My dear mother, if there is one thing more than another I dislike, it is a feather-bed. I should not be able to close my eyes; I beg of you to have it taken away."

Mrs Norton's face flushed. "I cannot under stand, John; it is absurd to say that you cannot sleep on a feather-bed. Mr Hare told me you complained of insomnia, and there is no surer way of losing your health. It is owing to the hardness of those college mattresses, whereas in a feather bed——"

"There is no use in our arguing that point, mother, I say I cannot sleep on a feather-bed. . . ."

"But you have not tried one; I don't believe you ever slept on a feather-bed in your life."

"Well, I am not going to begin now."

"We haven't another bed aired in the house, and it is really too late to ask the servants to change your room."

"Well, then, I shall be obliged to sleep at the hotel in Henfield."

"You should not speak to your mother in that way; I will not have it."

"There! you see we are quarrelling already; I did wrong to come home."

"I am speaking to you for your own good, my dear John, and I think it is very stubborn of you to refuse to sleep on a feather-bed; if you don't like it, you can change it to-morrow."

The conversation fell, and in silence the speakers strove to master their irritation. Then John, for politeness' sake, spoke of when he had last seen Kitty. It was about five years ago. She had ridden her pony over to see them.

Mrs Norton talked of some people who had left the county, of a marriage, of an engagement, of a mooted engagement; and she jerked in a suggestion that if John were to apply at once, he would be placed on the list of deputy-lieutenants. Enumeration of the family influence—Lord So-and-so, the cousin, was the Lord Lieutenant's most intimate friend.

"You are not even a J.P., but there will be no difficulty about that; and you have not seen any of the county people for years. We will have the carriage out some day this week, and we'll pay a round of visits."

"We'll do nothing of the kind. I have no time for visiting; I must get on with my book. I hope to finish my study of St Augustine before I leave here. I have my books to unpack, and a great deal of reading to get through. I have done no more than glance at the Anglo-Latin. Literature died in France with Gregory of Tours at the end of the sixth century; with St Gregory the Great, in Italy, at the commencement of the seventh century; in Spain about the same time. And then the Anglo-Saxons became the representatives of the universal literature. All this is most important.

I must re-read St Aldhelm and the Venerable Bede. . . . Now, I ask, do you expect me—me, with my head full of Aldhelm's alliterative verses—

'Turbo terram teretibus
Quæ catervatim cælitus
Neque cælorum culmina

. .   .   .

. .   .   .

Grassabatur turbinibus
Crebrantur nigris nubibus
Carent nocturna nebula—'

a letter descriptive of a great storm which he was caught in as he was returning home one night. . . ."

"Now, sir, we have had quite enough of that, and I would advise you not to go on with any of that nonsense here; you will be turned into dreadful ridicule."

"That's just why I wish to avoid them . . . but you have no pity for me. Just fancy my having to listen to them! How I have suffered. . . . What is the use of growing wheat when we are only getting eight pounds ten a load? . . . But we must grow something, and there is nothing else but wheat. We must procure a certain amount of straw, or we'd have no manure, and you can't work a farm without manure. I don't believe in the fish manure. But there is market gardening, and if we kept shops in Brighton, we could grow our own stuff and sell it at retail price. . . . And then there is a great deal to be done with flowers."

"Now, sir, that will do, that will do. . . . How dare you speak to me so! I will not allow it." And then relapsing into an angry silence, Mrs Norton drew her shawl about her shoulders.

One of a thousand quarrels. The basis of each nature was common sense—shrewd common sense—but such similarity of structure is in itself apt to lead to much violent shocking of opinion; and to this end an adjuvant was found in the dose of fantasy, mysticism, idealism which was inherent in John's character. "Why is he not like other people? Why will he waste his time with a lot of rubbishy Latin authors? Why will he not take up his position in the county?" Mrs Norton asked herself these questions as she fumed on the sofa.

"I wonder why she will continue to try to impose her will upon mine. I wonder why she has not found out by this time the uselessness of her effort. But no; she still keeps on hoping at last to wear me down. She wants me to live the life she has marked out for me to live—to take up my position in the county, and, above all, to marry and give an heir to the property. I see it all; that is why she wanted me to spend Christmas with her; that is why she has Kitty Hare here to meet me. How cunning, how mean women are: a man would not do that. Had I known it. . . . I have a mind to leave to-morrow. I wonder if the girl is in the little conspiracy." And turning his head he looked at her.

Tall and slight, a grey dress, pale as the wet sky, fell from her waist outward in the manner of a child's frock, and there was a lightness, there was brightness in the clear eyes. The intense youth of her heart was evanescent; it seemed constantly rising upwards like the breath of a spring morning—a morning when the birds are trilling. The face sharpened to a tiny chin, and the face was pale, although there was bloom on the cheeks. The forehead was shadowed by a sparkling cloud of brown hair, the nose was straight, and each little nostril was pink tinted. The ears were like shells. There was a rigidity in her attitude. She laughed abruptly, perhaps a little nervously, and the abrupt laugh revealed the line of tiny white teeth. Thin arms fell straight to the translucent hands, and there was a recollection of puritan England in look and in gesture. Her picturesqueness calmed John's ebullient discontent; he decided that she knew nothing of, and was not an accomplice in, his mother's scheme. For the sake of his guest he strove to make himself agreeable during dinner, but it was clear that he missed the hierarchy of the college table. The conversation fell repeatedly. Mrs Norton and Kitty spoke of making syrup for the bees; and their discussion of the illness of poor Dr——, who would no longer be able to get through the work of the parish single-handed, and would require a curate, was continued till the ladies rose from table. Nor did matters mend in the library. John's thoughts went back to his book; the room seemed to him intolerably uncomfortable and ugly. He went to the billiard-room to smoke a cigar. It was not clear to him if he would be able to spend two months in this odious place. He might offer them to God as penance for his sins; if every evening passed like the present, it were a modern martyrdom. But had they removed that horrid featherbed? He went upstairs. The feather-bed had been removed.

The room was large and ample, and it was draped with many curtains—pale curtains covered with walking birds and falling petals, a sort of Indian pattern. There was a sofa at the foot of the bed, and the toilette-table hung out its skirts in the wavering light of the fire. John tossed to and fro staring at the birds and petals. He thought of his ascetic college bed, of the great Christ upon the wall, of the prie-dieu with the great rosary hanging, but in vain; he could not rid his mind of the distasteful feminine influences which had filled the day, and which now haunted the night.

After breakfast next morning Mrs Norton stopped John as he was going upstairs to unpack his books. "Now," she said, "you must go out for a walk with Kitty Hare, and I hope you will make yourself agreeable. I want you to see the new greenhouse I have put up; she'll show it to you. And I told the bailiff to meet you in the yard. I thought you might like to see him."

"I wish, mother, you would not interfere in my business; had I wanted to see Burnes I should have sent for him."

"If you don't want to see him, he wants to see you. There are some cottages on the farm that must be put into repair at once. As for interfering in your business, I don't know how you can talk like that; were it not for me the whole place would be falling to pieces."

"Quite true; I know you save me a great deal of expense; but really . . ."

"Really what? You won't go out to walk with Kitty Hare?"

"I did not say I wouldn't, but I must say that I am very busy just now. I had thought of doing a little reading, for I have an appointment with my solicitor in the afternoon."

"That man charges you £200 a-year for collecting the rents; now, if you were to do it yourself, you would save the money, and it would give you something to do."

"Something to do! I have too much to do as it is. . . . But if I am going out with Kitty. . . . Where is she?"

"I saw her go into the library a moment ago."

And as it was preferable to go for a walk with Kitty than to continue the interview with his mother, John seized his hat and called Kitty, Kitty, Kitty! Presently she appeared, and they walked towards the garden, talking. She told him she had been at Thornby Place the whole time the greenhouse was being built, and when they opened the door they were greeted by Sammy. He sprang instantly on her shoulder.

"This is my cat," she said. "I've fed him since he was a little kitten; isn't he sweet?"

The girl was beautiful on the brilliant flower background; she stroked the great caressing creature, and when she put him down he mewed reproachfully. Further on her two tame rooks cawed joyously, and alighted on her shoulder.

"I wonder they don't fly away, and join the others in the trees."

"One did go away, and he came back nearly dead with hunger. But he is all right now, aren't you, dear?" And the bird cawed, and rubbed its black head against its mistress' cheek. "Poor little things, they fell out of the nest before they could fly, and I brought them up. But you don't care for pets, do you, John?"

"I don't like birds!"

"Don't like birds! Why, that seems as strange as if you said that you didn't like flowers."

"Mrs Norton told me, sir, that you would like to speak to me about them cottages on the Erring-ham Farm," said the bailiff.

"Yes, yes, I must go over and see them tomorrow morning at ten o'clock. I intend to go thoroughly into everything. How are they getting on with the cottages that were burnt down?"

"Rather slow, sir, the weather is so bad."

"But talking of fire, Burnes, I find that I can insure at a much cheaper rate at Lloyds' than at most of the offices. I find that I shall make a saving of £20 a-year."

"That's worth thinking about, sir."

While the young squire talked to his bailiff Kitty fed her rooks. They cawed, and flew to her hand for the scraps of meat. The coachman came to speak about oats and straw. They went to the stables. Kitty adored horses, it amused John to see her pat them, and her vivacity and light-heartedness rather pleased him than otherwise.

Nevertheless, during the whole of the following week the ladies held little communication with John. He lived apart from them. In the mornings he went out with his bailiffs to inspect farms and consult about possible improvement and necessary repairs. He had appointments with his solicitor. There were accounts to be gone through. He never paid a bill without verifying every item. It was difficult to say what should be done with a farm for which a tenant could not be found even at a reduced rent. At four o'clock he came into tea, his head full of calculations of such a complex character that even his mother could not follow the different statements to his satisfaction. When she disagreed with him, he took up the "Epistles of St Columban of Bangor," the "Epistola ad Sethum," or the celebrated poem, "Epistola ad Fedolium," written when the saint was seventy-two, and continued his reading, making copious notes in a pocket-book. To do so he drew his chair close to the library fire, and when Kitty came quickly into the room with a flutter of skirts and a sound of laughter, he awoke from contemplation, and her singing as she ascended the stairs jarred the dreams of cloister and choir which mounted from the pages to his brain in clear and intoxicating rhapsody.

On the third of November Mrs Norton announced that the meet of the hounds had been fixed for the fifteenth, and that there would be a hunt breakfast.

"Oh, my dear mother! you don't mean that they are coming here to lunch!"

"For the last twenty years all our side of the county has been in the habit of coming here to lunch, but of course you can shut your doors to all your friends and acquaintances. No doubt they will think you have come down here on purpose to insult them."

"Insult them! why should I insult them? I haven't seen them since I was a boy. I remember that the hunt breakfast used to go on all day long. Every woman in the county used to come, and they used to stay to tea, and you used to insist on a great number remaining to supper."

"Well, you can put a stop to all that now that you have consented to come to Thornby Place, only I hope you don't expect me to remain here to see my friends insulted."

"But just think of the expense! and in these bad times. You know I cannot find a tenant for the Woreington farm. I am afraid I shall have to provide the capital and farm it myself. Now, in the face of such losses, don't you think that we should retrench?"

"Retrench! A few fowls and rounds of beef! You don't think of retrenching when you present Stanton College with a stained glass window that costs five hundred pounds."

"Of course, if you like it, mother . . ."

"I like nothing but what you like, but I really think that for you to put down the hunt breakfast the first time you honour us with a visit, would look very much as if you intended to insult the whole county."

"It will be a day of misery for me!" replied John, laughing; "but I daresay I shall live through it."

"I think you will like it very much," said Kitty. "There will be a lot of pretty girls here: the Misses Green are coming from Worthing; the eldest is such a pretty girl, you are sure to admire her. And the hounds and horses look so beautiful."

Mrs Norton and Kitty spoke daily of invitations, and later on of cooking and the various things that were wanted. John continued to go through his accounts in the morning, and to read monkish Latin in the evening; but he was secretly nervous, and he dreaded the approaching day.

He was called an hour earlier—eight o'clock; he drank a cup of cold tea and ate a piece of dry toast in a back room. The dining-room was full of servants, who laid out a long table rich with comestibles and glittering with glass. Mrs Norton and Kitty were upstairs dressing.

He wandered into the drawing-room and viewed the dead, cumbrous furniture; the two cabinets bright with brass and veneer. He stood at the window staring. It was raining. The yellow of the falling leaves was hidden in the grey mist. It ceased to rain. "This weather will keep many away; so much the better; there will be too many as it is. I wonder who this can be." A melancholy brougham passed up the drive. There were three old maids, all looking sweetly alike; one was a cripple who walked with crutches, and her smile was the best and the gayest imaginable smile.

"How little material welfare has to do with our happiness," thought John. "There is one whose path is the narrowest, and she is happier and better than I." And then the three sweet old maids talked with their cousin of the weather; and they all wondered—a sweet feminine wonderment—if he would see a girl that day whom he would marry.

Presently the house was full of people. The passage was full of girls; a few men sat at breakfast at the end of the long table. Some red coats passed across the green glare of the park, and the hounds trotted about a single horseman. Voices. "Oh!

how sweet they look! oh, the dear dogs!" The huntsman stopped in front of the house, the hounds sniffed here and there, the whips trotted their horses and drove them back. "Get together, get together; get back there; Woodland, Beauty, come up here." The hounds rolled on the grass, and leaned their fore-paws on the railings, willing to be caressed.

"How sweet they are, look at their soft eyes," cried an old lady whose deity was a pug, and whose back garden reeked of the tropics. "Look how good and kind they are; they would not hurt anything; it is only wicked men who teach them to be . . ." The old lady hesitated before the word "bad," and murmured something about killing.

There was a lady with melting eyes, many children, and a long sealskin, and she availed herself of the excuse of seeing the hounds to rejoin a young man in whom she was interested. There was an old sportsman of seventy winters, as hale and as hearty as an oak, standing on the door-step, and he made John promise to come over and see him. The girls strolled about in groups. As usual young men were lacking. Looking at his watch, the huntsman pressed the sides of his horse, and rode to draw the covers at the end of the park. The ladies followed to see the start, although the mud was inches deep under foot. "Hu in, hu in," cried the huntsman. The whips trotted round cracking their long whips. Not a sound was heard. Suddenly there was a whimper, "Hark to Woodland," cried the huntsman. The hounds rallied to the point, but nothing came of it. Apparently the old bitch was at fault. The huntsman muttered something inaudible. But some few hundred yards further on, in an outlying clump where no one would expect to find, a fox broke clean away.

The country is as flat as a smooth sea. Chanctonbury Ring stands up like a mighty cliff on a northern shore; its crown of trees is grim. The abrupt ascents of Toddington Mount bear away to the left, and tide-like the fields flow up into the great gulf between.

"He's making for the furze, but he'll never reach them; he got no start, and the ground is heavy."

Then the watchers saw the horsemen making their way up the chalky roads cut in the precipitous side of the downs. Rain began to fall, umbrellas were put up, and all hurried home to lunch.

"Now John, try and make yourself agreeable, go over and talk to some of the young ladies. Why do you dress yourself in that way? Have you no other coat? You look like a young priest. Look at that young man over there! how nicely dressed he is! I wish you would let your moustache grow; it would improve you immensely." With these and similar remarks whispered to him, Mrs Norton continued to exasperate her son until the servants announced that lunch was ready. "Take in Mrs So-and-so," she said to John, who would fain have escaped from the melting glances of the lady in the long sealskin. He offered her his arm with an air of resignation, and set to work valiantly to carve a huge turkey.

As soon as the servants had cleared away after one set another came, and although the meet was a small one, John took six ladies in to lunch. About half-past three the men adjourned to the billiard-room to smoke. The girls, mighty in numbers, followed, and, with their arms round each other's waists, and interlacing fingers, they grouped themselves about the room. Two huntsmen returned dripping wet, and much to his annoyance, John had to furnish them with a change of clothes. There was tea in the drawing-room about five o'clock, and soon after the visitors began to take their leave.

The wind blew very coldly, the roosting rooks rose out of the branches, and the carriages rolled into the night; but still a remnant of visitors stood on the steps talking to John. His cold was worse; he felt very ill, and now a long sharp pain had grown through his left side, and momentarily it became more and more difficult to exchange polite words and smiles. The footmen stood waiting by the open door, the horses champed their bits, the green of the park was dark, and a group of kissing girls moved about the loggia, wheels grated on the gravel . . . all were gone! The butler shut the door, and John went to the library fire.

There his mother found him. She saw that something was seriously the matter. He was helped up to bed, and the doctor was sent for. A bad attack of pleurisy. John was rolled up in an enormous mustard plaster—mustard and cayenne pepper; it bit into the flesh. He roared with pain; he was slightly delirious; he cursed those around him, using blasphemous language.

For more than a week he suffered. He lay bent over, unable to straighten himself, as if a nerve had been wound up too tightly in the left side. He was fed on gruel and beef-tea, the room was kept very warm; it was not until the twelfth day that he was taken out of bed.

"You have had a narrow escape," the doctor said to John, who, well wrapped up, lay back, looking very weak and pale, before a blazing fire. "It was very lucky I was sent for. Twenty-four hours later I would not have answered for your life."

"I was delirious, was I not?"

"Yes, slightly; you cursed and swore fearfully at us when we rolled you up in the mustard plaster. . . . Well, it was very hot, and must have burnt you."

"Yes, it was; it has scarcely left a bit of skin on me. But did I use very bad language? I suppose I could not help it. ... I was delirious, was I not?"

"Yes, slightly."

"Yes; but I remember, and if I remember right, I used very bad language; and people when they are really delirious do not know what they say. Is not that so, doctor?"

"If they are really delirious they do not remember, but you were only slightly delirious . . . you were maddened by the pain occasioned by the pungency of the plaster."

"Yes; but do you think I knew what I was saying?"

"You must have known what you were saying, because you remember what you said."

"But could I be held accountable for what I said?"

"Accountable. . . . Well, I hardly know what you mean. You were certainly not in the full possession of your senses. Your mother (Mrs Norton) was very much shocked, but I told her that you were not accountable for what you said."

"Then I could not be held accountable, I did not know what I was saying."

"I don't think you did exactly; people in a passion don't know what they say!"

"Ah! yes, but we are answerable for sins committed in the heat of passion: we should restrain our passion; we were wrong in the first instance in giving way to passion. . . . But I was ill, it was not exactly passion. And I was very near death; I had a narrow escape, doctor?"

"Yes, I think I can call it a narrow escape."

The voices ceased,—five o'clock,—the curtains were rosy with lamp light, and conscience awoke in the langours of convalescent hours. "I stood on the verge of death!" The whisper died away. John was still very weak, and he had not strength to think with much insistance, but now and then remembrance surprised him suddenly like pain; it came unexpectedly, he knew not whence nor how, but he could not choose but listen. Each interval of thought grew longer; the scabs of forgetfulness were picked away, the red sore was exposed bleeding and bare. Was he responsible for those words? He could remember them all now; each like a burning arrow lacerated his bosom, and he pulled them to and fro. Remembrance in the watches of the night, dawn fills the dark spaces of a window, meditations grow more and more lucid. He could now distinguish the instantaneous sensation of wrong that had flashed on his excited mind in the moment of his sinning. . . . Then he could think no more, and in the twilight of contrition he dreamed vaguely of God's great goodness, of penance, of ideal atonements. Christ hung on the cross, and far away the darkness was seared with flames and demons.

And as strength returned, remembrance of his blasphemies grew stronger and fiercer, and often as he lay on his pillow, his thoughts passing in long procession, his soul would leap into intense suffering. "I stood on the verge of death with blasphemies on my tongue. I might have been called to confront my Maker with horrible blasphemies in my heart and on my tongue; but He in His Divine goodness spared me: He gave me time to repent. Am I answerable, O my God, for those dreadful words that I uttered against Thee, because I suffered a little pain, against Thee Who once died on the cross to save me! O God, Lord, in Thine infinite mercy look down on me, on me! Vouchsafe me Thy mercy, O my God, for I was weak! My sin is loathsome; I prostrate myself before Thee, I cry aloud for mercy!"

Then seeing Christ amid His white million of youths, beautiful singing saints, gold curls and gold aureoles, lifted throats, and form of harp and dulcimer, he fell prone in great bitterness on the misery of earthly life. His happinesses and ambitions appeared to him less than the scattering of a little sand on the sea-shore. Joy is passion, passion is suffering; we cannot desire what we possess, therefore desire is rebellion prolonged indefinitely against the realities of existence; when we attain the object of our desire, we must perforce neglect it in favour of something still unknown, and so we progress from illusion to illusion. The winds of folly and desolation howl about us; the sorrows of happiness are the worst to bear, and the wise soon learn that there is nothing to dream of but the end of desire. . . . God is the one ideal, the Church the one shelter from the misery and meanness of life. Peace is inherent in lofty arches, rapture in painted panes. . . . See the mitres and crosiers,

the blood-stained heavenly breasts, the loin-linen hanging over orbs of light. . . .
Listen! ah! the voices of chanting boys, and out of the cloud of incense come Latin
terminations, and the organ still is swelling.

In such religious æstheticisms the soul of John Norton had long slumbered,
but now it awoke in remorse and pain, and, repulsing its habitual exaltations even
as if they were sins, he turned to the primal idea of the vileness of this life, and its
sole utility in enabling man to gain heaven. Beauty, what was it but temptation?
He winced before a conclusion so repugnant to him, but the terrors of the verge on
which he had so lately stood were still upon him in all their force, and he crushed
his natural feelings. . . .

The manifestation of modern pessimism in John Norton has been described,
and how its influence was checked by constitutional mysticity has also been shown.
Schopenhauer, when he overstepped the line ruled by the Church, was instantly rejected. From him John Norton's faith had suffered nothing; the severest and
most violent shocks had come from another side—a side which none would guess,
so complex and contradictory are the involutions of the human brain. Hellenism,
Greek culture and ideal; academic groves; young disciples, Plato and Socrates, the
august nakedness of the Gods were equal, or almost equal, in his mind with the lacerated bodies of meagre saints; and his heart wavered between the temple of simple
lines and the cathedral of a thousand arches. Once there had been a sharp struggle,
but Christ, not Apollo, had been the victor, and the great cross in the bedroom of
Stanton College overshadowed the beautiful slim body in which Divinity seemed to
circulate like blood; and this photograph was all that now remained of much youthful anguish and much temptation.

A fact to note is that his sense of reality had always remained in a rudimentary
state; it was, as it were, diffused over the world and mankind. For instance, his belief in the misery and degradation of earthly life, and the natural bestiality of man,
was incurable; but of this or that individual he had no opinion; he was to John Norton a blank sheet of paper, to which he could not affix even a title. His childhood
had been one of bitter tumult and passionate sorrow; the different and dissident
ideals growing up in his heart and striving for the mastery, had torn and tortured
him, and he had long lain as upon a mental rack. Ignorance of the material laws of
existence had extended even into his sixteenth year, and when, bit by bit, the veil

fell, and he understood, he was filled with loathing of life and mad desire to wash himself free of its stain; and it was this very hatred of natural flesh that precipitated a perilous worship of the deified flesh of the God. But mysticity saved him from plain paganism, and the art of the Gothic cathedral grew dear to him. It was nearer akin to him, and he assuaged his wounded soul in the ecstacies of incense and the great charms of Gregorian chant.

But fear now for the first time took possession of him, and he realised—if not in all its truth, at least in part—that his love of God had only taken the form of a gratification of the senses, a sensuality higher but as intense as those which he so much reproved. Fear smouldered in his very entrails, and doubt fumed and went out like steam—long lines and falling shadows and slowly dispersing clouds. His life had been but a sin, an abomination, and the fairest places darkened as the examination of conscience proceeded. His thought whirled in dreadful night, soul-torturing contradictions came suddenly under his eyes, like images in a night-mare; and in horror and despair, as a woman rising from a bed of small-pox drops the mirror after the first glance, and shrinks from destroying the fair remembrance of her face by pursuing the traces of the disease through every feature, he hid his face in his hands and called for forgiveness—for escape from the endless record of his conscience. With staring eyes and contracted brows he saw the flames which await him who blasphemes. To the verge of those flames he had drifted. If God in His infinite mercy had not withheld him? . . He pictured himself lost in fires and furies. Then looking up he saw the face of Christ, grown pitiless in final time—Christ standing immutable amid His white million of youths. . . .

And the worthlessness and the abjectness of earthly life struck him with awful and all-convincing power, and this vision of the worthlessness of existence was clearer than any previous vision. He paused. There was but one conclusion . . . it looked down upon him like a star—he would become a priest. All darkness, all madness, all fear faded, and with sure and certain breath he breathed happiness; the sense of consecration nestled in its heart, and its light shone upon his face.

There was nothing in the past, but there is the sweetness of meditation in the present, and in the future there is God. Like a fountain flowing amid a summer of leaves and song, the sweet hours came with quiet and melodious murmur. In the great arm-chair of his ancestors he sits thin and tall. Thin and tall. The great flames decorate the darkness, and the twilight sheds upon the rose curtains, walking birds and falling petals. But his thoughts are dreaming through long aisle and solemn arch, clouds of incense and painted panes. . . The palms rise in great curls like the sky; and amid the opulence of gold vestments, the whiteness of the choir, the Latin terminations and the long abstinences, the holy oil comes like a kiss that never dies . . . . and in full glory of symbol and chant, the very savour of God descends upon him . . . and then he awakes, surprised to find such dreams out of sleep.

His resolve did not alter; he longed for health because it would bring the realisation of his desire, and time appeared to him cruelly long. Nor could he think of the pain he inflicted on his mother, so centred was he in this thought; he was blind to her sorrowing face, he was deaf to her entreaty; he could neither feel nor see beyond the immediate object he had in mind, and he spoke to her in despair of the length of months that separated him from consecration; he speculated on the possibility of expediting that happy day by a dispensation from the Pope, The moment he could obtain permission from the doctor he ordered his trunks to be packed, and when he bid Mrs Norton and Kitty Hare goodbye, he exacted a promise from the former to be present at Stanton College on Palm Sunday. He wished her to be present when he embraced Holy Orders.

CHAPTER IV.

EVERY morning Mrs Norton flung her black shawl over her shoulders, rattled her keys, and scolded the servants at the end of the long passage. Kitty, as she watered the flowers in the greenhouse, often wondered why John had chosen to become a priest and grieve his mother. Three times out of five when the women met at lunch, Mrs Norton said:

"Kitty, would you like to come out for a drive?"

Kitty answered, "I don't mind; just as you like, Mrs Norton."

After tea at five Kitty read for an hour, and in the evening she played the piano; and she sometimes endeavoured to console her hostess by suggesting that people did change their minds, and that John might not become a priest after all. Mrs Norton looked at the girl, and it was often on her lips to say, "If you had only flirted, if you had only paid him some attentions, all might have been different." But heart-broken though she was, Mrs Norton could not speak the words. The girl looked so candid, so flowerlike in her guilelessness, that the thought seemed a pollution. And in a few days Mr Hare sent for Kitty; and with her departed the last ray of sunlight, and Thornby Place grew too sad and solitary for Mrs Norton.

She went to visit some friends; she spent Christmas at the Rectory; and in the long evenings when Kitty had gone to bed, she opened her heart to her old friend. The last hope was gone; there was nothing for her to look for now. John did not even write to her; she had not heard from him since he left. It was very wrong of the Jesuits to encourage him in such conduct, and she thought of laying the whole matter before the Pope. The order had once been suppressed; she did not remember by what Pope; but a Pope had grown tired of their intrigues, and had suppressed the order. She made these accusations in moments of passion, and immediately after came deep regret. . . . How wrong of her to speak ill of her religion, and to a Protestant! If John did become a priest it would be a punishment for her sins. But what was she saying? If John became a priest, she should thank God for His great goodness. What greater honour could he bestow upon her? Next day she took the train to Brighton, and went to confession; and that very same evening she plead-ingly suggested to Mr Hare that he should go to Stanton College, and endeavour to persuade John to return home. The parson was of course obliged to decline. He advised her to leave the matter in the hands of God, and Mrs Norton went to bed a prey to scruples of conscience of all kinds.

She even began to think it wrong to remain any longer in an essentially Prot-estant atmosphere. But to return to Thornby Place alone was impossible, and she begged for Kitty. The parson was loth to part with his daughter, but he felt there was much suffering beneath the calm exterior that Mrs Norton preserved. He could refuse her nothing, and he let Kitty go.

"There is no reason why you should not come and dine with us every day; but I shall not let you have her back for the next two months."

"What day will you come and see us, father dear?" said Kitty, leaning out of the carriage window.

"On Thursday," cried the parson.

"Very well, we shall expect you," replied Mrs Norton; and with a sigh she sank back on the cushions, and fell to thinking of her son.

At Thornby Place everything was soon discovered to be in a sad state of ne-glect. There was much work to be clone in the greenhouse, the azaleas were being devoured by insects, and the leaves required a thorough washing. It was easy to see that the cats had not been regularly fed, and one of the tame rooks had flown away. Remedying these disasters, Mrs Norton and Kitty hurried to and fro. There was a ball at Steyning, and Mrs Norton consented to do the chaperon for once; and the girl's dress was a subject of gossip for a month—for a fortnight an absorbing oc-cupation. Most of the people who had been at the hunt breakfast were at the ball, and Kitty had plenty of partners. These suggested husbands to Mrs Norton, and she questioned Kitty; but she did not seem to have thought of the ball except in the light of a toy which she had been allowed to play with one evening. The young men she had met there had apparently interested her no more than if they had been girls, and she regretted John only because of Mrs Norton. Every morning she ran to see if there was a letter, so that it might be she who brought the good news. But no letter came. Since Christmas John had written two short notes, and now they were well on in April. But one morning as she stood watching the springtide, Kitty saw him walking up the drive; the sky was growing bright with blue, and the beds were catching flower beneath the evergreen oaks. She ran to Mrs Norton, who. was at-tending to the canaries in the bow-window.

"Look, look, Mrs Norton, John is coming up the drive; it is he; look!"

"John!" said Mrs Norton, seeking for her glasses nervously; "yes, so it is; let's run and meet him. But no; let's take him rather coolly. I believe half his eccentricity is only put on because he wishes to astonish us. We won't ask him any questions; we'll just wait and let him tell his own story. . . ."

"How do you do, mother?" said the young man, kissing Mrs Norton with less reluctance than usual. "You must forgive me for not having answered your letters. It really was not my fault; I have been passing through a very terrible state of mind lately. . . . And how do you do, Kitty? Have you been keeping my mother company ever since? It is very good in you; I am afraid you must think me a very undutiful son. But what is the news?

"One of the rooks is gone."

"Is that all? . . . What about the ball at Steyning? I hear it was a great success."

"Oh, it was delightful."

"You must tell me about it after dinner. Now I must go round to the stables and tell Walls to take the trap round to the station to fetch my things."

"Are you going to be here some time?" said Mrs Norton, assuming an indifferent air.

"Yes, I think so; that is to say, for a couple of months—six weeks. I have some arrangements to make, but I will speak to you about all that after dinner."

With these words John left the room, and he left his mother agitated and frightened.

"What can he mean by having arrangements to make?" she asked. Kitty could of course suggest no explanation, and the women waited the pleasure of the young man to speak his mind. He seemed, however, in no hurry to do so; and the manner in which he avoided the subject aggravated his mother's uneasiness. At last she said, unable to bear the suspense any longer:

"Are you going to be a priest, John, dear?"

"Of course, but not a Jesuit. . . ."

"And why? have you had a quarrel with the Jesuits?"

"Oh, no; never mind; I don't like to talk about it; not exactly a quarrel, but I have seen a great deal of them lately, and I have found them out. I don't mean in anything wrong, but the order is so entirely opposed to the monastic spirit. It is difficult to explain; I really can't . . . What I mean is . . . well, that their worldliness is repugnant to me—fashionable friends, confidences, meddling in family affairs, dining out, letters from ladies who need consolation. . . . I don't mean anything wrong; pray don't misunderstand me. I merely mean to say that I hate their meddling in family affairs. Their confessional is a kind of marriage bureau; they have always got some plan on for marrying this person to that, and I must say I hate all that sort of thing. ... If I were a priest I would disdain to . . . but perhaps I am wrong to speak like that. Yes, it is very wrong of me, and before . . . Kitty, you must not think I am speaking against the principles of my religion, I am only speaking of matters of——"

"And have you given up your rooms in Stanton College?"

"Not yet; that is to say, nothing is settled definitely, but I do not think I shall go back there; at least not to live."

"And you still are determined on becoming a priest?"

"Certainly, but not a Jesuit."

"What then?

"A Carmelite. I have seen a great deal of these monks lately, and it is only they who preserve some of the old spirit of the old ideal. To enter the Carmelite Chapel in Kensington is to step out of the mean atmosphere of to-day into the lofty charm of the Middle Ages. The long straight folds of habits falling over sandalled feet, the great rosaries hanging down from the girdles, the smell of burning wax, the large tonsures, the music of the choir; I know nothing like it. Last Sunday I heard them sing St Fortunatus' hymn, . . . the ***Vexilla regis*** heard in the cloud of incense, and the wrath of the organ! . . . splendid are the rhymes! the first stanza in U and O, the second in A, and the third in E; passing over the closed vowels, the hymn ascends the scale of sound——"

"Now, John, none of that nonsense; how dare you, sir? Don't attempt to laugh at your mother."

"My dear mother, you must not think I am sneering because I speak of what is uppermost in my mind. I have determined to become a Carmelite monk, and that is why I came down here."

Mrs Norton was very angry; her temper fumed, and she would have burst into violent words had not the last words, "and that is why I came down here," frightened her into calmness.

"What do you mean?" she said, turning round in her chair. "You came down here to become a Carmelite monk; what do you mean?"

John hesitated. He was clearly a little frightened, but having gone so far he felt he must proceed. Besides, to-day, or to-morrow, sooner or later the truth would have to be told. He said:

"I intend altering the house a little here and there; you know how repugnant this mock Italian architecture is to my feelings I am coming to live here with some monks——"

"You must be mad, sir; you mean to say that you intend to pull down the house of your ancestors and turn it into a monastery?"

John drew a breath of relief, the worst was over now; she had spoken the fulness of his thought. Yes, he was going to turn Thornby Place into a monastery.

"Yes," he said, "if you like to put it in that way. Yes, I am going to turn Thornby Place into a monastery. Why shouldn't I? I am resolved never to marry; and I have no one except those dreadful cousins to leave the place to. Why shouldn't I turn it into a monastery and become a monk? I wish to save my soul."

Mrs Norton groaned.

"But you make me say more than I mean. To turn the place into a Gothic monastery, such a monastery as I dreamed would not be possible, unless indeed I pulled the whole place down, and I have not sufficient money to do that, and I do not wish to mortgage the property. For the present I am determined only on a few alterations. I have them all in my head. The billiard room, that addition of yours, can be turned into a chapel. And the casements of the dreadful bow-window might be removed, and mullions and tracery fixed on, and, instead of the present flat roof, a sloping tiled roof might be carried up against the wall of the house. The cloisters would come at the back of the chapel."

John stopped aghast at the sorrow he was causing, and he looked at his mother. She did not speak. Her ears were full of merciless ruins; hope vanished in the white dust; and the house with its memories sacred and sweet fell pitilessly: beams lying this way and that, the piece of exposed wall with the well-known wall paper, the crashing of slates. How they fall! John's heart was rent with grief, but he could not stay his determination any more than his breath. Youth is a season of suffering, we cannot surrender our desire, and it lies heavy and burning on our hearts. It is so easy for age, so hard for youth to make sacrifices. Youth is and must be wholly, madly selfish; it is not until we have learnt the folly of our aims that we may forget them, that we may pity the sufferings of others, that we may rejoice in the triumphs of our friends. To the superficial therefore, John Norton will appear but the incarnation of egotism and priggishness, but those who see deeper will have recognised that he is one who has suffered bitterly, as bitterly as the outcast who lies dead in his rags beneath the light of the policeman's lantern. Mental and physical wants!—he who may know one may not know the other: is not the absence of one the reason of the other? Mental and physical wants! the two planes of suffering whence the great divisions of mankind view and envy the other's destinies, as we view a passing pageant, as those who stand on the decks of crossing ships gaze regretfully back.

Those who have suffered much physical want will never understand John Norton; he will find commiseration only from those who have realised à priori the worthlessness of existence, the vileness of life; above all, from those who, conscious of a sense of life's degradation, impetuously desire their ideal—the immeasurable ideal which lies before them, clear, heavenly, and crystalline; the sea into which they would plunge their souls, but in whose benedictive waters they may only dip their fingertips, and crossing themselves, pass up the aisle of human tribulation. We suffer in proportion to our passions. But John Norton had no passion, say they who see passion only in carnal dissipation. Yet the passions of the spirit are more terrible than those of the flesh; the passion for God, the passion of revolt against the humbleness of life; and there is no peace until passion of whatever kind has wailed itself out.

Foolish are they who describe youth as a time of happiness; it is one of fever and anguish.

Beneath its apparent calm, there was never a stormier youth than John's. The boy's heart that grieves to death for a chorus-girl, the little clerk who mourns to madness for the bright life that flashes from the point of sight of his high office stool, never felt more keenly the nervous pain of desire and the lassitudes of resistance. You think John Norton did not suffer in his imperious desire to pull down the home of his fathers and build a monastery! Mrs Norton's grief was his grief, but to stem the impulse that bore him along was too keen a pain to be endured. His desire whelmed him like a wave; it filled his soul like a perfume, and against his will it rose to his lips in words. Even when the servants were present he could not help discussing the architectural changes he had determined upon, and as the vision of the cloister, with its reading and chanting monks, rose to his head, he talked, blinded by strange enthusiasm, of latticed windows, and sandals.

His mother bit her thin lips, and her face tightened in an expression of settled grief. Kitty was sorry for Mrs Norton, but Kitty was too young to understand, and her sorrow evaporated in laughter. She listened to John's explanations of the future as to a fairy tale suddenly touched with the magic of realism. That the old could not exist in conjunction with the new order of things never grew into the painful precision of thought in her mind. She saw but the show side; she listened as to an account of private theatricals, and in spite of Mrs Norton's visible grief, she was amused when John described himself walking at the head of his monks with tonsured head and a great rosary hanging from a leather girdle. Her innocent gaiety attracted her to him. As they walked about the grounds after breakfast, he spoke to her about pictures and statues, of a trip he intended to take to Italy and Spain, and he did not seem to care to be reminded that this jarred with his project for immediate realisation of Thornby Priory.

Leaning their backs against the iron railing which divided the green sward from the park, John and Kitty looked at the house.

"From this view it really is not so bad, though the urns and the loggia are so intolerably out of keeping with the landscape. But when I have made my alterations it will harmonise with the downs and the flat-flowing country, so English with its barns and cottages and rich agriculture, and there will be then a charming recollection of old England, the England of the monastic ages, before the—but I forgot, I must not speak to you on that subject."

"Do you think the house will look prettier than it does now? Mrs Norton says that it will be impossible to alter Italian architecture into Gothic. . . . Of course I don't understand."

"Mother does not know what she is talking about. I have it all down in my pocket-book. I have various plans. ... I admit it is not easy, but last night I fancy I hit on an idea. I shall of course consult an architect, although really I don't see there is any necessity for so doing, but just to be on the safe side; for in architecture there are many practical difficulties, and to be on the safe side I will consult an experienced man regarding the practical working out of my design. I made this drawing last night." John produced a large pocket-book.

"But, oh, how pretty; will it be really like that?"

"Yes," exclaimed John, delighted; "it will be exactly like that; but I will read you my notes, and then you will understand it better.

"Alter and add to the front to represent the facade of a small cathedral. This can he done by building out a projection the entire width of the building, and one storey in height. This will be divided, into three arched divisions, topped with small gables."

"What are gables, John?"

"Those are the gables. The centre one (forming entrance) being rather higher than the other gables. The entrance would be formed with clustered columns and richly moulded pointed arches, the door being solid, heavy oak, with large scroll and, hammered iron hinges.

"The centre front and, back would, be carried up to form steep gables, the roof being heightened, to match. The large gable in front to have a large cross at apex."

"What is an apex? What words you do use."

John explained, Kitty laughed.

"The top I have indicated in the drawing. *And to have a rose window.* You see the rose window in the drawing," said John, anticipating the question which was on Kitty's lips.

"Yes," said she, "but why don't you say a round window?"

Without answering John continued:

"The first floor fronts would he arcaded round with small columns with carved capitals and pointed arches.

"At either corner of front, in lieu of present Ionic columns, carry up octagonal turrets with pinnacles at top.

"You see them in the drawing. These are the octagonal turrets."

"And which are the pinnacles?"

"The ornaments at the top.

"From the centre of the roof carry up a square tower with battlemented parapets and pinnacles at all corners, and flying buttresses from the turrets of the main buildings.

"The bow window at side will have the old casements removed, and have mullions and tracery fixed and filled with cathedral glazings, and, instead of the present flat, a sloping roof will be carried up and finished against the outer wall of the house. At either side of bay window buttresses with moulded water-tables, plinths, &c.

"From these roofs and the front projections at intersection of small gables, carved gargoyles to carry off water.

"The billiard-room to be converted into a chapel, by building a new high-pitched, roof."

"Oh, John, why should you do away with the billiard-room; why shouldn't the monks play billiards? You played billiards on the day of the meet."

"Yes, but I am not a monk yet. No one ever heard of monks playing billiards; besides, that dreadful addition of my mother's could not remain in its present form, it would be ludicrous to a degree, whereas it can be converted very easily into a chapel. We must have a chapel—***building a high-pitched timber roof, throwing out an apse at the end, and "putting in mullioned and traceried windows filled with stained glass"***

"And the cloister you are always speaking about, where will that be?"

"The cloister will come at the back of the chapel, and an arched and vaulted ambulatory will be laid round the house. Later on I shall add a refectory, and put a lavatory at one end of the ambulatory."

"But don't you think, John, you may get tired of being a monk, and then the house will have to be built back again."

"Never, the house will be from every point of view, a better house when my alterations are carried into effect. Beside, why should I be tired of being a monk? Your father does not get tired of being a parson."

This reply, although singularly unconvincing, was difficult to answer, and the conversation fell. And day by day, John's schemes strengthened and took shape, and he seemed to look upon him self already as a Carmelite. He had even gone so far as to order a habit, it had arrived a few days ago; and an architect, too, had come down from London. He was the ray of hope in Mrs Norton's life. For although he had loudly commended the artistic taste exhibited in the drawing, and expressed great wonderment at John's architectural skill, he had, nevertheless, when questioned as to their practicability, declared the scheme to be wholly impossible. And the reasons he advanced in support of his opinions were so conclusive that John was fain to beg of him to draw up a more possible plan for the conversion of an Italian house into a Gothic monastery.

Mr——seemed to think the idea a wild one, but he promised to see what could be done to overcome the difficulties he foresaw, and in a week he forwarded John several drawings for his consideration. Judged by comparison with John's dreams, the practical architecture of the experienced man seemed altogether lacking in expression and in poetry of proportion; and comparing them with his own cherished project, John hung over the billiard-table, where the drawings were laid out, hour after hour, only to rise more bitterly fretful, more utterly unable than usual to reconcile himself to natural limitation, more hopelessly longing for the unattainable.

He could think of nothing but his monastery; his Latin authors were forgotten; he drew façades and turrets on the cloth during dinner, and he went up to his room, not to bed, but to reconsider the difficulties that rendered the construction of a central tower an impossibility.

Midnight: the house seems alive in the silence: night is on the world. The twilight sheds on the walking birds, on the falling petals, and in the rich shadow the candle burns brightly. The great bridal bed yawns, the lace pillows lie wide, the curtains hang dreamily in the hallowed light. John leans over his drawings. Once again he takes up the architect's notes.

"The interior would be so constructed as to make it impossible to carry up the central tower. The outer walls would not be strong enough to take the large gables and roof. Although the chapel could be done easily^ the ambulatory would be of no use, as it would lead probably from the kitchen offices.

"Would have to reduce work on front façade to putting in new arched entrance. Buttresses would take the place of columns.

"The bow-window could remain.

"The roof to be heightened somewhat. The front projection would throw the front rooms into almost total darkness."

"But why not a light timber lantern tower?" thought John. "Yes, that would get over the difficulty. Now if we could only manage to keep my front . . . if my design for the front cannot be preserved, I might as well abandon the whole thing! And then?"

And then life seemed to him void of meaning and light. He might as well settle down and marry. . . .

His face contracted in an expression of anger. He rose from the table, and he looked round the room. Its appearance was singularly jarring, shattering as it did his dream of the cloister, and up-building in fancy the horrid fabric of marriage and domesticity. The room seemed to him a symbol—with the great bed, voluptuous, the corpulent arm-chair, the toilet-table shapeless with muslin—of the hideous laws of the world and the flesh, ever at variance and at war, and ever defeating the indomitable aspirations of the soul. John ordered his room to be changed; and, in the face of much opposition from his mother, who declared that he would never be able to sleep there, and would lose his health, he selected a narrow room at the end of the passage. He would have no carpet. He placed a small iron bed against the wall; two plain chairs, a screen to keep off the draught from the door, a basin-stand such as you might find in a ship's cabin, and a prie-dieu, were all the furniture he permitted himself.

"Oh, what a relief! he murmured. "Now there is line, there is definite shape. That formless upholstery frets my eye as false notes grate on my ear; "and, becoming suddenly conscious of the presence of God, he fell on his knees and prayed. He prayed that he might be guided aright in his undertaking, and that, if it were conducive to the greater honour and glory of God, he might be permitted to found a monastery, and that he might be given strength to surmount all difficulties.

Next morning, calm in mind, and happier, he went downstairs to the drawing-room, a small book in his hand, an historical work of great importance by the Venerable Bede, intitled Vita beatorum abbatum Wiremuthensim, et Girvensiuem, Benedicti Ceolfridi, Easteriwini, Sigfridi atque Hœtherti. But he could not keep his attention fixed on the book, it appeared to him dreary and stupid. His thoughts wandered. He thought of Kitty—of how beautiful she looked on the background of red geraniums, with the soft yellow cat on her shoulder, and he wondered which of the four great painters, Manet, Degas, Monet, or Renoir would have best rendered the brightness and lightness, the intense colour vitality of that motive for a picture. He thought of her young eyes, of the pale hands, of the sudden, sharp laugh; and finally he took up one of her novels, "Red as a Rose is She." He read it, and found it very entertaining.

But the evening post brought him a letter from the architect's head clerk, saying that Mr——was ill, had not been to the office for the last three or four days, and would not be able to go down to Sussex again before the end of the month. Very much annoyed, John spent the evening thinking whom he could consult on the practicability of his last design for the front, and next morning he was surprised at not seeing Kitty at breakfast.

"Where is Kitty?" he asked abruptly.

"She is not feeling well; she has a headache, and will not be down to-day."

At the end of a long silence, John said:

"I think I will go into Brighton. . . . I must really see an architect."

"Oh, John, dear, you are not really determined to pull the house down?"

"There is no use, mother dear, in our discussing that subject; each and all of us must do the best we can with life. And the best we can do is to try and gain heaven."

"Breaking your mother's heart, and making yourself ridiculous before the whole county, is not the way to gain heaven."

"Oh, if you are going to talk like that. . . ."

John went into the drawing-room to continue his reading, but the Latin bored him even more than it had done yesterday. He took up the novel, but its enchantment was gone, and it appeared to him in its tawdry, original vulgarity. He got on a horse and rode towards the downs, and went up the steep ascents at a gallop. He stood amid the gorse at the top and viewed the great girdle of blue encircling sea, and the long string of coast towns lying below him, and far away. Lunch was on the table when he returned. After lunch, harassed by an obsession of architectural plans, he went out to sketch. But it rained, and resisting his mother's invitation to change his clothes, he sat down before the fire, damp without, and feverishly irritable within. He vacillated an hour between his translation of St Fortunatus' hymn, Quern terra, pontus œthera, and "Red as a Rose is She," which, although he thought it as reprehensible for moral as for literary reasons, he was fain to follow out to the vulgar end. But he could interest himself in neither hymn nor novel. For the authenticity of the former he now cared not a jot, and he threw the book aside vowing that its hoydenish heroine was unbearable and he would read no more.

"I never knew a more horrible place to live in than Sussex. Either of two things: I must alter the architecture of this house, or I must return to Stanton College."

"Don't talk nonsense, do you think I don't know you? you are boring yourself because Kitty is upstairs in bed, and cannot walk about with you."

"I do not know how you contrive, mother, always to say the most disagreeable possible things; the marvellous way in which you pick out what will, at the moment, wound me most is truly wonderful. I compliment you on your skill, but I confess I am at a loss to understand why you should, as if by right, expect me to remain here to serve continuously as a target for the arrows of your scorn."

John walked out of the room. During dinner mother and son spoke very little, and he retired early, about ten o'clock, to his room. He was in high dudgeon, but the white walls, the prie-dieu, the straight, narrow bed were pleasant to see. His room was the first agreeable impression of the day. He picked up a drawing from the table, it seemed to him awkward and slovenly. He sharpened his pencil, cleared his crow-quill pens, got out his tracing-paper, and sat down to execute a better. But he had not finished his outline sketch before he leaned back in his chair, and as if overcome by the insidious warmth of the fire, lapsed into fire-light attitudes and meditations.

He looked a little backwards into the blaze; he nibbled his pencil point. Wavering light and wavering shade followed fast over the Roman profile, followed and flowed fitfully—fitfully as his thoughts. Now his thought followed out architectural dreams, and now he thought of himself, of his unhappy youth, of how he had been misunderstood, of his solitary life; a bitter, unsatisfactory life, and yet a life not wanting in an ideal—a glorious ideal. He thought how his projects had always met with failure, with disapproval, above all failure . . . . and yet, and yet he felt, he almost knew there was something great and noble in him. His eyes brightened; he slipped into thinking of schemes for a monastic life; and then he thought of his mother's hard disposition and how she misunderstood him,—everyone misunderstood him. What would the end be? Would he succeed in creating the monastery he dreamed of so fondly? To reconstruct the ascetic life of the Middle Ages, that would be something worth doing, that would be a great ideal—that would make meaning in his life. If he failed . . . . what should he do then? His life as it was, was unbearable .... he must come to terms with life. . . .

That central tower! how could he manage it! and that built-out front. Was it true, as the architect said, that it would throw all the front rooms into darkness? Without this front his design would be worthless. What a difference it made!

Kitty liked it. She had thought it charming. How young she was, how glad and how innocent, and how clever, her age being taken into consideration. She understood all you said. It would not surprise him if she developed into something: but she would marry. . . .

But why was he thinking of her? What concern had she in his life? A little slip of a girl—a girl—a girl more or less pretty, that was all. And yet it was pleasant to hear her laugh. That low, sudden laugh—she was pleasanter company than his mother, she was pleasant to have in the house, she interrupted many an unpleasant scene. Then he remembered what his mother had said. She had said that he was disappointed that she was ill, that he had missed her, that . . . . that it was because she was not there that he had found the day so intolerably wearisome.

Struck as with a dagger, the pain of the wound flowed through him piercingly; and as a horse stops and stands trembling, for there is something in the darkness beyond, John shrank back, his nerves vibrating like highly-strung chords; and ideas—notes of regret and lamentation died in great vague spaces. Ideas fell. . . . Was this all; was this all he had struggled for; was he in love? A girl, a girl . . . was a girl to soil the ideal he had in view? No; he smiled painfully. The sea of his thoughts grew calmer, the air grew dim and wan, a tall foundered wreck rose pale and spectral, memories drifted. The long walks, the talks of the monastery, the neighbours, the pet rooks, and Sammy the great yellow cat, and the green-houses . . . he remembered the pleasure he had taken in those conversations!

What must all this lead to? To a coarse affection, to marriage, to children, to general domesticity.

And contrasted with this . . . .

The dignified and grave life of the cloister, the constant sensation of lofty and elevating thought, a high ideal, the communion of learned men, the charm of headship.

Could he abandon this? No, a thousand times no; but there was a melting sweetness in the other cup. The anticipation filled his veins with fever.

And trembling and pale with passion, John fell on his knees and prayed for grace. But prayer was sour and thin upon his lips, and he could only beg that the temptation might pass from him. . . .

"In the morning," he said, "I shall be strong,"

CHAPTER V.

BUT if in the morning he were strong, Kitty was more beautiful than ever, and they walked out in the sunlight. They walked out on the green sward, under the evergreen oaks where the young rooks are swinging; out on the mundane swards into the pleasure ground; a rosery and a rockery; the pleasure ground divided from the park by iron railings, the park encircled by the rich elms, the elms shutting out the view of the lofty downs.

The meadows are yellow with buttercups, and the birds fly out of the gold. And the golden note is prolonged through the pleasure grounds by the pale yellow of the laburnums, by the great yellow of the berberis, by the cadmium yellow of the gorse, by the golden wallflowers growing amid rhododendrons and laurels.

And the transparent greenery of the limes shivers, and the young rooks swinging on the branches caw feebly.

And about the rockery there are purple bunches of lilac, and the striped awning of the tennis seat touches with red the paleness of the English spring.

Pansies, pale yellow pansies!

The sun glinting on the foliage of the elms spreads a napery of vivid green, and the trunks come out black upon the cloth of gold, and the larks fly out of the gold, and the sky is a single sapphire, and two white clouds are floating. It is May time.

They walked toward the tennis seat with its red striped awning. They listened to the feeble cawing of young rooks swinging on the branches. They watched the larks nestle in, and fly out of the gold. It was May time, and the air was bright with buds and summer bees. She was dressed in white, and the shadow of the straw hat fell across her eyes when she raised her face. He was dressed in black, and the clerical frock coat buttoned by one button at the throat fell straight.

They sat under the red striped awning of the tennis seat. The large grasping hands holding the polished cane contrasted with the reedy translucent hands laid upon the white folds. The low sweet breath of the May time breathed within them, and their hearts were light; hers was conscious only of the May time, but his was awake with unconscious love, and he yielded to her, to the perfume of the garden, to the absorbing sweetness of the moment. He was no longer John Norton. His being was part of the May time; it had gone forth and had mingled with the colour of the fields and sky; with the life of the flowers, with all vague scents and sounds; with the joy of the birds that flew out of and nestled with amorous wings in the gold. Enraptured and in complete forgetfulness of his vows, he looked at her, he felt his being quickening, and the dark dawn of a late nubility radiated into manhood.

"How beautiful the day is," he said, speaking slowly. "Is it not all light and colour, and you in your white dress with the sunlight on your hair seem more blossom-like than any flower. I wonder what flower I should compare you to. . . . Shall I say a rose? No, not a rose, nor a lily, nor a violet; you remind me rather of a tall delicate pale carnation. . . ."

"Why, John, I never heard you speak like that before; I thought you never paid compliments."

The transparent green of the limes shivers, the young rooks caw feebly, and the birds nestle with amorous wings in the blossoming gold. Kitty has taken off her straw hat, the sunlight caresses the delicate plenitudes of the bent neck, the delicate plenitudes bound with white cambric, cambric swelling gently over the bosom into the narrow circle of the waist, cambric fluted to the little wrist, reedy translucid hands; cambric falling outwards and flowing like a great white flower over the green sward, over the mauve stocking, and the little shoe set firmly. The ear is as a rose leaf, a fluff of light hair trembles on the curving nape, and the head is crowned with thick brown gold. "O to bathe my face in those perfumed waves! O to kiss with a deep kiss the hollow of that cool neck! . . ." The thought came he know not whence nor how, as lightning falls from a clear sky, as desert horsemen come with a glitter of spears out of the cloud; there is a shock, a passing anguish, and they are gone.

He left her. So frightened was he at this sudden and singular obsession of his spiritual nature by a lower and grosser nature, whose existence in himself was till now unsuspected, and of whose life and wants in others he had felt, and still felt, so much scorn, that in the tumult of his loathing he could not gain the calm of mind necessary for an examination of conscience. He could not look into his mind with any present hope of obtaining a truthful reply to the very eminent and vital question, how far his will had participated in that burning but wholly inexcusable desire by which he had been so shockingly assailed.

That inner life, so strangely personal and pure, and of which he was so proud, seemed to him now to be befouled, and all its mystery and inner grace, and the perfect possession which was his sanctuary, lost to him for ever. For he could never quite forget the defiling thought; it would always remain with him, and the consciousness of the stain would preclude all possibility of that refining happiness, that attribute of cleanliness, which he now knew had long been his. In his anger and self-loathing his rage turned against Kitty. It was always the same story—the charm and ideality of man's life always soiled by woman's influence; so it was in the beginning, so it shall be. . . .

He stopped before the injustice of the accusation; he remembered her candour and her gracious innocence, and he was sorry; and he remembered her youth and her beauty, and he let his thoughts dwell upon her. Turning over his papers he came across the old monk's song to David:

"Surge meo domno dulces fac, fistula versus: David amat versus, surge fac fistula versus, David amat vates vatornm est gloria David. . . ."

The verses seemed meaningless and tame, but they awoke vague impulses in him, and, his mind filled by a dim dream of King David and Bathsheba, he opened his Bible and turned over the pages, reading a phrase here and there until he had passed from story and psalm to the Song of songs, and was finally stopped by—"I charge you, O daughters of Jerusalem, if ye find my beloved, that ye tell him that I am sick of love."

He laid the book down and leaned back in his chair, and holding his temple with one hand (this was his favourite attitude) he looked in the fire fixedly. He was ravaged by emotion. The magical fervour of the words he had just read had revealed to him the depth of his passion.

But he would tear the temptation out of his heart. The conduct of his life had been long-ago determined upon. He had known the truth as if by instinct from the first; no life was possible except an ascetic life, at least for him. And in this hour of weakness he summoned to his aid all his ancient ideals: the solemnity and twilight of the arches, the massive Gregorian chant which seems to be at once their voice and their soul, the cloud of incense melting upon the mitres and sunsets, and the boys' treble hovering over an ocean of harmony. But although the picture of his future life rose at his invocation it did not move him as heretofore, nor did the scenes he evoked of conjugal grossness and platitude shock him to the extent he had expected. The moral rebellion he succeeded in exciting was tepid, heartless, and ineffective, and he was not moved by hate or fear until he remembered that God in His infinite goodness had placed him for ever out of the temptation which he so earnestly sought to escape from. Kitty was a Protestant. In a pang of despair, windows and organ collapsed like cardboard; incense and arches vanished, and then rose again with the light of a more gracious vision upon them. For if the dignity and desire of mere self-salvation had departed, all the lighter colours and livelier joys of the conversion of others filled the sky of faith with morning tones and harmonies. And then? . . . Salvation before all things, he answered in his enthusiasm;—something of the missionary spirit of old time was upon him, and forgetful of his aisles, his arches, his Latin authors, he went down stairs and asked Kitty to play a game of billiards.

"We play billiards here on Sunday, but you would think it wrong to do so."

"But to-day is not Sunday."

"No, I was only speaking in a general way. Yet I often wonder how you can feel satisfied with the protection your Church affords you against the miseries and trials of the world. A Protestant, you know, may believe pretty nearly as little or as much as he likes, whereas in our church everything is defined; we know what we must believe to be saved. There is a sense of security in the Catholic Church which the Protestant has not."

"Do you think so? That is because you do not know our Church," replied Kitty, who was a little astonished at this sudden outburst. "I feel quite happy and safe. I know that our Lord Jesus Christ died on the Cross to save us, and we have the Bible to guide us."

"Yes, but the Bible without the interpretation of the Church is . . . may lead to error. For instance . . ."

John stopped abruptly. Seized with a sudden scruple of conscience he asked himself if he, in his own house, had a right to strive to undermine the faith of the daughter of his own friend.

"Go on," cried Kitty, laughing, "I know the Bible better than you, and if I break down I will ask father. And as if to emphasise her intention, she hit her ball which was close under the cushion as hard as she could.

John hailed the rent in the cloth as a deliverance, for in the discussion as to how it could be repaired, the religious question was forgotten.

But if he were her lover, if she were going to be his wife, he would have the right to offer her every facility and encouragement to enter the Catholic Church— the true faith. Darkness passes, and the birds are carolling the sun, flowers and trees are pranked with aerial jewellery, the fragrance of the warm earth flows in your veins, your eyes are fain of the light above and your heart of the light within. He would not jar his happiness by the presence of Mrs Norton, even Kitty's presence was too actual a joy to be borne. She drew him out of himself too completely, interrupted the exquisite sense of personal enchantment which seemed to permeate and flow through him with the sweetness of health returning to a convalescent on a spring day. He closed his eyes, and his thoughts came and went like soft light and shade in a garden close; his happiness was a part of himself, as fragrance is inherent in the summer time. The evil of the last days had fallen from him, and the reaction was equivalently violent. Nor was he conscious of the formal resignation he was now making of his dream, nor did he think of the distasteful load of marital duties with which he was going to burden himself; all was lost in the vision of beautiful companionship, a sort of heavenly journeying, a bright earthly way with flowers and starlight—he a little in advance pointing, she following, with her eyes lifted to the celestial gates shining in the distance. Sometimes his arms would be thrown about her. Sometimes he would press a kiss upon her face. She was his, his, and he was her saviour. The evening died, the room darkened, and John's dream continued in the twilight, and the ringing of the dinner bell and the disturbance of dressing did not destroy his thoughts. Like fumes of wine they hung about him during the evening, and from time to time he looked at Kitty.

But although he had so far surrendered himself, he did not escape without another revulsion of feeling. A sudden realisation of what his life would be under the new conditions did not fail to frighten him, and he looked back with passionate regret on his abandoned dreams. But his nature was changed, abstention he knew was beyond his strength, and after many struggles, each of which was feebler than the last, he determined to propose to Kitty on the first suitable occasion.

Then came the fear of refusal. Often he was paralysed with pain, sometimes he would morbidly allow his thoughts to dwell on the moment when he would hear her say, it was impossible, that she did not and could not love him. The young grey light of the eyes would be fixed upon him; she would speak her sorrow, and her thin hands would hang by her side in the simple attitude that was so peculiar to her. And he mused willingly on the long meek life of grief that would then await him. He would belong to God; his friar's frock would hide all; it would be the habitation, and the Gothic walls he would raise, the sepulchre of his love. . . .

"But no, no, she shall be mine," he cried out, moved in his very entrails. Why should she refuse him? What reason had he to believe that she would not have him? He thought of how she had answered his questions on this and that occasion, how she had looked at him; he recalled every gesture and every movement with wonderful precision, and then he lapsed into a passionate consideration of the general attitude of mind she evinced towards him. He arrived at no conclusion, but these meditations were full of penetrating delight. Sometimes he was afflicted with an intense shyness, and he avoided her; and when Mrs Norton, divining his trouble, sent them to walk in the garden, his heart warmed to his mother, and he regretted his past harshness.

And this idyll was lived about the beautiful Italian house, with its urns and pilasters; through the beautiful English park, with its elms now with the splendour of summer upon them; in the pleasure grounds with their rosary, and the fountain where the rose leaves float, and the wood-pigeons come at eventide to drink; in the greenhouse with its live glare of geraniums, where the great yellow cat, so soft and beautiful, springs on Kitty's shoulder, rounds its back, and purring, insists on caresses; in the large clean stables where the horses munch the corn lazily, and look round with round inquiring eyes, and the rooks croak and flutter, and strut about Kitty's feet. It was Kitty; yes, it was Kitty everywhere; even the blackbird darting through the laurels seemed to cry Kitty.

To propose! Time, place, and the words he should use had been carefully considered. After each deliberation, a new decision had been taken: but when he came to the point, John found himself unable to speak any one of the different versions he had prepared. Still he was very happy. The days were full of sunshine and Kitty, and he mistook her light-heartedness for affection. He had begun to look upon her as his certain wife, although no words had been spoken that would suggest such a possibility. Outside of his imagination nothing was changed; he stood in exactly the same relation to her as he had done when he returned from Stanton College, determined to build a Gothic monastery upon the ruins of Thornby Place, and yet somehow he found it difficult to realise that this was so.

One morning he said, as they went into the garden, "You must sometimes feel a little lonely here . . . when I am away . . . all alone here with mother."

"Oh dear no! we have lots to do. I look after the pets in the morning. I feed the cats and the rooks, and I see that the canaries have fresh water and seed. And then the bees take up a lot of our time. We have twenty-two hives. Mrs Norton says she ought to make five pounds a year on each. Sometimes we lose a swarm or two, and then Mrs Norton is so cross. We were out for hours with the gardener the other day, but we could do no good; we could not get them out of that elm tree. You see that long branch leaning right over the wall; well it was on that branch that they settled, and no ladder was tall enough to reach them; and when Bill climbed the tree and shook them out they flew right away."

"Shall I, shall I propose to her now?" thought John. But Kitty continued talking, and it was difficult to interrupt her. The gravel grated under their feet; the rooks were flying about the elms. At the end of the garden there was a circle of fig trees. A silent place, and John vowed he would say the word there. But as they approached his courage died within him, and he was obliged to defer his vows until they reached the green-house.

"So your time is fully occupied here."

"And in the afternoon we go out for drives; we pay visits. You never pay visits; you never go and call on your neighbours."

"Oh, yes I do; I went the other day to see your father."

"Ah yes, but that is only because he talks to you about Latin authors."

"No, I assure you it isn't. Once I have finished my book I shall never look at them again."

"Well, what will you do?"

"Next winter I intend to go in for hunting. I have told a dealer to look out for a couple of nice horses for me."

Kitty looked up, her grey eyes wide open. If John had told her that he had given the order for a couple of crocodiles she could not have been more surprised.

"But hunting is over now; it won't begin again till next November. You will have to play lawn tennis this summer."

"I have sent to London for a racquet and shoes, and a suit of flannels."

"Goodness me. . . . Well, that is a surprise! But .you won't want the flannels; you might play in the Carmelite's habit which came down the other day. How you do change your mind about things!"

"Do you never change your mind, Kitty?"

"Well, I don't know, but not so suddenly as you. Then you are not going to become a monk?"

"I don't know, it depends on circumstances."

"What circumstances?" said Kitty, innocently.

The words *"whether you will or will not have me"* rose to John's lips, but all power to speak them seemed to desert him; he had grown suddenly as weak as melting snow, and in an instant the occasion had passed. He hated himself for his weakness. The weary burden of his love lay still upon him, and the torture of utterance still menaced him from afar. The conversation had fallen. They were approaching the greenhouse, and the cats ran to meet their patron. Sammy sprang on Kitty's shoulder.

"Oh, isn't he a beauty? stroke him, do."

John passed his hand along the beautiful yellow fur. Sammy rubbed his head against his mistress' face, her raised eyes were as full of light as the pale sky, and the rich brown head and the thin hands made a picture in the exquisite clarity of the English morning,—in the homeliness of the English garden, with tall hollyhocks, espalier apple trees, and one labourer digging amid the cabbages. Joy crystal as the morning itself illumined John's mind for a moment, and then faded, and he was left lonely with the remembrance that his fate had still to be decided, that it still hung in the scale.

One evening as they were walking in the park, shadowy in the twilight of an approaching storm, Kitty said:

"I never would have believed, John, that you could care to go out for a walk with me."

"And why, Kitty?"

Kitty laughed—her short sudden laugh was strange and sweet. John's heart was beating. "Well," she said, without the faintest hesitation or shyness, "we always thought you hated girls. I know I used to tease you, when you came home for the first time; when you used to think of nothing but the Latin authors."

"What do you mean?"

Kitty laughed again.

"You promise not to tell?"

"I promise."

This was their first confidence.

"You told your mother when I came, when you were sitting by the fire reading, that the flutter of my skirts disturbed you."

"No, Kitty, I'm sure you never disturbed me, or at least not for a long time. I wish my mother would not repeat conversations, it is most unfair."

"Mind you, you promised not to repeat what I have told you. If you do, you will get me into an awful scrape."

"I promise."

The conversation came to a pause. Presently Kitty said, "But you seem to have got over your dislike to girls. I saw you talking a long while with Miss Orme the other day; and at the Meet you seemed to admire her. She was the prettiest girl we had here."

"No, indeed she wasn't!"

"Who was, then?"

"You were."

Kitty looked up; and there was so much astonishment in her face that John in a sudden access of fear said, "We had better make haste, the storm is coming on; we shall get wet through."

They ran towards the house. John reproached himself bitterly, but he made no further attempt to screw his courage up to the point' of proposing. His disappointment was followed by doubts. Was his powerlessness a sign from God that he was abandoning his true vocation for a false one? and a little shaken, he attempted to interest himself in the re-building of his house; but the project had grown impossible to him, and he felt he could not embrace it again, with any of the old enthusiasm at least, until he had been refused by Kitty. There were moments when he almost yearned to hear her say that she could never love him. But in his love and religious suffering the thought of bringing a soul home to the true fold remained a fixed light; he often looked to it with happy eyes, and then if he were alone he fell on his knees and prayed. Prayer like an opiate calmed his querulous spirit, and having told his beads—the great beads which hung on his prie-dieu—he would go down stairs with peace in his heart, and finding Kitty, he would ask her to walk with him in the garden, or they would stroll out on the tennis lawn, racquet in hand.

One afternoon it was decided that they should go for a long walk. John suggested that they should climb to the top of Toddington Mount, and view the immense plain which stretches away in dim blue vapour and a thousand fields.

You see John and Kitty as they cross the wide park towards the vista in the circling elms,—she swinging her parasol, he carrying stiffly his grave canonical cane. He still wears the long black coat buttoned at the throat, but the air of hieratic dignity is now replaced by, or rather it is glossed with, the ordinary passion of life. Both are like children, infinitely amused by the colour of the grass and sky, by the hurry of the startled rabbit, by the prospect of the long walk; and they taste already the wild charm of the downs, seeing and hearing in imagination its many sights and sounds, the wild heather, the yellow savage gorse, the solitary winding flock, the tinkling of the bell-wether, the cliff-like sides, the crowns of trees, the mighty distance spread out like a sea below them with its faint and constantly dissolving horizon of the Epsom Hills.

"I never can cross this plain, Kitty, without thinking of the Dover cliffs as seen in mid Channel; this is a mere inland imitation of them."

"I have never seen the Dover cliffs; I have never been out of England, but the Brighton cliffs give me an idea of what you mean."

"On your side—the Shoreham side—the downs rise in a gently sloping ascent from the sea."

"Yes, we often walk up there. You can see Brighton and Southwick and Worthing. Oh! it is beautiful! I often go for a walk there with my friends, the Austen girls—you saw them here at the Meet."

"Yes, Mr Austen has a very nice property; it extends right into the town of Shoreham, does it not?"

"Yes, and right up to Toddington Mount, where we are going. But aren't you a little tired, John? These roads are very steep."

"Out of breath, Kitty; let's stop for a minute or two." The country lay below them. They had walked three miles, and Thornby Place and its elms were now vague in the blue evening. "We must see one of these days if we cannot do the whole distance."

"What? right across the downs from Shoreham to Henfield?"

"Well, it is not more than eight miles; you don't think you could manage it?"

"I don't know, it is more than eight miles, and walking on the downs is not like walking on the highroad. Father thinks nothing of it."

"We must really try it."

"What would you do if I were to get so tired that I could not go back or forward?"

"I would carry you."

They continued their climb. Speaking of the Devil's Dyke, Kitty said—

"What! you mean to say you never heard the legend? You, a Sussex man!"

"I have lived very little in Sussex, and I used to hate the place; I am only just beginning to like it."

"And you don't like the Jesuits any more, because they go in for matchmaking."

"They are too sly for me, I confess; I don't approve of priests meddling in family affairs. But tell me the legend."

"Oh, how steep these roads are. At last, at last. Now let's try and find a place where we can sit down. The grass is full of that horrid prickly gorse."

"Here's a nice soft place; there is no gorse here. Now tell me the legend."

"Well, I never!" said Kitty, sitting herself on the spot that had been chosen for her, "you do astonish me. You never heard of the legend of St Cuthman."

"No, do tell it to me."

"Well, I scarcely know how to tell it in ordinary words, for I learnt it in poetry."

"In poetry! In whose poetry?"

"Evy Austen put it into poetry, the eldest of the girls, and they made me recite it at the harvest supper."

"Oh, that's awfully jolly—I never should have thought she was so clever. Evy is the dark-haired one."

"Yes, Evy is awfully clever; but she doesn't talk much about it."

"Do recite it."

"I don't know that I can remember it all. You won't laugh if I break down."

"I promise."

THE LEGEND OF ST CUTHMAN.

"St Cuthman stood on a point which crowns The entire range of the grand South Downs; Beneath his feet, like a giant field, Was stretched the expanse of the Sussex Weald. 'Suppose,' said the Saint, ' 'twas the will of Heaven To cause this range of hills to be riven, And what were the use of prayers and winnings, Were the sea to flood the village of Poynings: 'Twould be fine, no doubt, these Downs to level, But to do such a thing I defy the Devil!' St Cuthman, tho' saint, was a human creature, And his eye, a bland and benevolent feature, Remarked the approach of the close of day, And he thought of his supper, and turned away. Walking fast, he Had scarcely passed the First steps of his way, when he saw something nasty; 'Twas tall and big, And he saw from its rig 'Twas the Devil in full diabolical fig. There were wanting no proofs, For the horns and the hoofs And the tail were a fully convincing sight; But the heart of the Saint Ne'er once turned faint, And his halo shone with redoubled light. 'Hallo, I fear You're trespassing here!' Said St Cuthman, 'To me it is perfectly clear, If you talk of the devil, he's sure to appear!' 'With my spade and my pick I am come,' said old Nick, 'To prove you've no power o'er a demon like me. I'll show you my power— Ere the first morning hour Thro' the Downs, over Poynings, shall roll in the sea.' 'I'll give you long odds,' Cried the Saint, 'by the gods! I'll stake what you please, only say what your wish is.' Said the devil, 'By Jove! You're a sporting old cove! My pick to your soul, I'll make such a hole, That where Poynings now stands, shall be swimming the fishes.' ' Done!' cried the Saint, 'but I must away I have a penitent to confess; In an hour I'll come to see fair play— In truth I cannot return in less. My bet will be won ere the first bright ray Heralds the ascension of the day. If I lose!—there will be ***the devil to pay!*** He descended the hill with a firm quick stride, Till he reached a cell which stood on the side; He knocked at the door, and it opened wide,— He murmured a blessing and walked inside. Before him he saw a tear-stained face Of an elderly maiden of elderly grace; Who, when she beheld him, turned deadly pale, And drew o'er her features a nun's black veil. 'Holy father!' she said, 'I have one sin more, Which I should have confessed sixty years before! I have broken my vows—'tis a terrible crime! I have loved ***you,*** oh father, for all that time! My passion I cannot subdue, tho' I try! Shrive me, oh father! and let me die!' 'Alas, my daughter,' replied the Saint, 'One's desire is ever to do what one mayn't, There was once a time when I loved you, too, I have conquered my passion, and why shouldn't you? For penance I say, You must kneel and pray For hours which will number seven; Fifty times say the rosary, (Fifty, 'twill be a poser, eh? But by it you'll enter heaven; As each hour doth pass, Turn the hour glass, Till the time of midnight's near; On the stroke of midnight This taper light, Your conscience will then be clear.' He left the cell, and he walked until He joined Old Nick on the top of the hill. It was five o'clock, and the setting sun Showed the work of the Devil already begun. St Cuthman was rather fatigued by his walk, And caring but little for brimstone talk, He watched the pick crash through layers of chalk. And huge blocks went over and splitting asunder Broke o'er the Weald like the crashing of thunder. St Cuthman wished the first hour would pass, When St Ursula, praying, reversed the glass. 'Ye legions of hell!' the Old Gentleman cried, 'I have such a terrible stitch in the side!' 'Don't work so hard,' said the Saint, 'only see, The sides of your dyke a heap smoother might be.' 'Just so,' said the Devil, 'I've had a sharp fit, So, resting, I'll trim up my crevice a bit.' St Cuthman was looking prodigiously sly, He knew that the hours were slipping by. 'Another attack! I've cramp at my back! I've needles and pins From my hair to my shins! I tremble and quail From my horns to my tail! I will not be vanquished, I'll work, I say, This dyke shall be finished ere break of day!' 'If you win your bet, 'twill be fairly earned,' Said the Saint, and again was the hour-glass turned. And then with a most unearthly din The farther end of the dyke fell in; But in spite of an awful rheumatic pain The Devil began his work again. 'I'll not be vanquished!' exclaimed the old bloke. 'By breathing torrents of flame and smoke, Your dyke,' said the Saint, 'is hindered each minute, What can one expect when the Devil is in it?' Then an accident happened, which caused Nick at last To rage, fume, and swear; when the fourth hour had passed, On his hoof there came rolling a huge mass of quartz. Then quite out of sorts The bad tempered old cove Sent the huge mass of stone whizzing over to Hove. He worked on again, till a howl and a cry Told the Saint one more hour—the fifth—had gone by. 'What's the row?' asked the Saint, 'A cramp in the wrist, I think for a while I had better desist.' Having rested a bit he worked at his chasm, Till, the hour having passed, he was seized with a spasm. He raged and he cursed, 'I bore this at first, The rheumatics were awful, but this is the worst.' With awful rage heated, The demon defeated, In his passion used words that can't be repeated. Feeling shaken and queer, In spite of his fear, At the dyke he worked on until midnight drew near. But when the glass turned for the last time, he found That the head of his pick was stuck fast in the ground. 'Cease now!' cried St Cuthman, 'vain is your toil! Come forth from the dyke! Leave your pick in the soil! You agreed to work 'tween sunset and morn, And lo! the glimmer of day is born! In vain was your fag, And your senseless brag.' Dizzy and dazed with sulphureous vapour, Old Nick was deceived by St Ursula's taper. 'The dawn!' yelled the Devil, 'in vain was my boast, That I'd have your soul, for I've lost it, I've lost!' 'Away!' cried St Cuthman, 'Foul fiend! away! See yonder approaches the dawn of day! Return to the flames where you were before, And molest these peaceful South Downs no more!' The old gentleman scowled but dared not stay, And the prints of his hoofs remain to this day, Where he spread his dark pinions and soared away. At St Ursula's cell Was tolling the bell, And St Cuthman in sorrow, stood there by her side. 'Twas over at last, Her sorrows were past, In the moment of triumph St Ursula died. Tho' this was the ground, There never were found The tools of the Devil, his spade and his pick; But if you want proof Of the Legend, the hoof- Marks are still in the hillock last trod by Old Nick."

"Oh! that is jolly. Well, I never thought the girl was clever enough to write that. And there are some excellent rhymes in it, 'passed he ' rhyming with ' nasty/ and ' rosary ' with ' poser, eh;' and how well you recite it."

"Oh, I recited it better at the harvest supper; and you have no idea how the farmers enjoyed it. They know the place so well, and it interested them on that account. They understood it all."

John sat as if enchanted,—by Kitty's almost childish grace, her enthusiasm for her friend's poem, and her genuine enjoyment of it; by the abrupt hills, mysterious now in sunset and legend; by the vast plains so blue and so boundless: out of the thought of the littleness of life, of which they were a symbol, there came the thought of the greatness of love.

"Won't you cross the poor gipsy's palm with a bit of silver, my pretty gentleman, and she will tell you your fortune and that of your pretty lady?"

Kitty uttered a startled cry, and turning they found themselves facing a strong, black-eyed girl. She repeated her question.

"What do you think, Kitty, would you like to have your fortune told?"

Kitty laughed. "It would be rather fun," she said.

She did not know what was coming, and she listened to the usual story, full by the way of references to John—of a handsome young man who would woo her, win her, and give her happiness, children, and wealth.

John threw the girl a shilling. She withdrew. They watched her passing through the furze. The silence about them was immense. Then John spoke:

"What the gipsy said is quite true; I did not dare to tell yon so before."

"What do you mean, John?"

"I mean that I am in love with you, will you love me?"

"You in love with me, John; it is quite absurd—I thought you hated girls."

"Never mind that, Kitty, say you will have me; make the gipsy's words come true."

"Gipsies' words always come true."

"Then you will marry me?"

"I never thought about marriage. When do you want me to marry you? I am only seventeen?"

"Oh! when you like, later on, only say you will be mine, that you will be mistress of Thornby Place one day, that is all I want."

"Then you don't want to pull the house down any more."

"No, no; a thousand times no! Say you will be my wife one of these days."

"Very well then, one of these days . . . ."

"And I may tell my mother of your promise to-night? ... It will make her so happy."

"Of course you may tell her, John, but I don't think she will believe it."

"Why should she not believe it?"

"I don't know," said Kitty, laughing, "but how funny, was it not, that the gipsy girl should guess right?"

"Yes, it was indeed. I wanted to tell you before, but I hadn't the courage; and I might never have found the courage if it had not been for that gipsy."

In his abundant happiness John did not notice that Kitty was scarcely sensible of the importance of the promise she had given. And in silence he gazed on the landscape, letting it sink into and fix itself for ever in his mind. Below them lay the great green plain, wonderfully level, and so distinct were its hedges that it looked like a chessboard. Thornby Place was hidden in vapour, and further away all was lost in darkness that was almost night.

"I am sorry we cannot see the house—your house," said John as they descended the chalk road.

"It seems so funny to hear you say that, John."

"Why? It will be your house some day."

"But supposing your Church will not let you marry me, what then . . . ."

"There is no danger of that; a dispensation can always be obtained. But who knows. . . You have never considered the question. . . . You know nothing of our Church; if you did, you might become a convert. I wish you would consider the question. It is so simple; we surrender our own wretched understanding, and are content to accept the Church as wiser than we. Once man throws off restraint there is no happiness, there is only misery. One step leads to another; if he would be logical he must go on, and before long, for the descent is very rapid indeed, he finds himself in an abyss of darkness and doubt, a terrible abyss indeed, where nothing exists, and life has lost all meaning. The Reformation was the thin end of the wedge, it was the first denial of authority, and you see what it has led to—modern scepticism and modern pessimism."

"I don't know what it means, but I heard Mrs Norton say you were a pessimist."

"I was; but I saw in time where it was leading me, and I crushed it out. I used to be a Republican too, but I saw what liberty meant, and what were its results, and I gave it up."

"So you gave up all your ideas for Catholicism. . . ."

John hesitated, he seemed a little startled, but he answered, "I would give up anything for my Church. . ."

"What! Me?"

"That is not required."

"And did it cost you much to give up your ideas?"

John raised his eyes—it was a look that Balzac would have understood and would have known how to interpret in some admirable pages of human suffering. "None will ever know how I have suffered," he said sadly. "But now I am happy, oh! so happy, and my happiness would be complete if. . . . Oh! if God would grant you grace to believe. . . ."

"But I do believe. I believe in our Lord Christ who died to save us. Is not that enough?"

CHAPTER VI.

LIKE Juggernaut's car, Catholicism had passed over John's mind, crushing all individualism, and leaving it but a wreck of quaking mysticism. Twenty times a day the spectre of his conscience rose and with menacing finger threatened him with flames and demons. And his love was a source of continual suffering. How often did he ask himself if he were surrendering his true vocation? How often did he beg of God to guide him aright? But these mental agitations were visible to no one. He preserved his calm exterior and the keenest eye detected in him only an ordinary young man with more than usually strict business habits. He had appointments with his solicitor. He consulted with him, he went into complex calculations concerning necessary repairs, and he laid plans for the more advantageous letting of the farms.

IIis mother encouraged him to attend to his business. Her head was full of other matters. A dispensation had to be obtained; it was said that the Pope was more than ever opposed to mixed marriages. But no objection would be made to this one. It would be madness to object. . . . A rich Catholic family at Henfield—nearly four thousand a-year—must not be allowed to become extinct. Thornby Place was the link between the Duke of Norfolk and the So and So's. If those dreadful cousins came in for the property, Protestantism would again be established at Thornby Place. And what a pity that would be; and just at a time when Catholicism was beginning to make headway in Sussex. And if John did not marry now he would never marry; of that she was quite sure.

As may be imagined, these were not the arguments with which Mrs Norton sought to convince the Rev. William Hare; they were those with which she besieged the Brompton Oratory, Farm Street, and the Pro-Cathedral. She played one off against the other. The Jesuits were nettled at having lost him, but it was agreeable to learn that the Carmelites had been no less unfortunate than they. The Oratorians on the whole thought he was not in their "line"; and as their chance of securing him was remote, they agreed that John would prove more useful to the Church as a married man than as a priest. A few weeks later the Papal sanction was obtained.

The clause concerning the children affected Mr Hare deeply, but he was told that he must not stand in the way of the happiness of two young people. He considered the question from many points of view, but in the meantime Mrs Norton continued to deluge Kitty with presents, and to talk to everybody of her son's marriage. The parson's difficulties were thereby increased, and eventually he found he could not withhold his consent.

And as time went on, John seemed to take a more personal delight in life than he had done before. He forgot his ancient prejudices if not his ancient ideals, and, as was characteristic of him, he avoided thinking with any definiteness on the nature of the new life into which he was to enter soon. His neighbours declared he was very much improved; and there were dinner parties at Thornby Place. One of his great pleasures was to start early in the morning, and having spent a long day with Kitty, to return home across the downs. The lofty, lonely landscape, with its lengthy hills defined upon the flushes of July, came in happy contrast with the noisy hours of tennis and girls; and standing on the gently ascending slopes, rising almost from the wicket gate of the rectory, he would wave farewells to Kitty and the Austins. And in the glittering morning, grey and dewy, when he descended these slopes to the strip of land that lies between them and the sea, he would pause on the last verge where the barn stands. Squire Austin's woods are in front, and they stretch by the town to the sleepy river with its spiderlike bridge crossing the sandy marshes. The church spire and roofs show through each break in the elm trees, and higher still the horizon of the sea is shimmering.

The rectory is rich brown brick and tiles. About it there is an ample farmyard. Mr Hare has but the house and an adjoining field, the three great ricks are Mr Austin's; the sunlight is upon them, and through the long shadows the cart horses are moving with the drays; and now a hundred pigeons rise and are seen against the green velvet of the elms, and one bird's wings are white upon the white sea.

Mr Hare is sitting in the verandah smoking, Kitty is attending to her birds.

"Good morning, John," she cried, "but I can't shake hands with you, my hands are dirty. Do you talk to father, I haven't a moment. There is such a lot to do. You know the Miss Austins are coming here to early dinner, and we have two young men coming from Worthing to play tennis. The court isn't marked yet."

"I will help you to mark it."

"Very well, but I am not ready yet."

John lit a cigar, and he spoke of books to Mr Hare, whom he considered a gross Philistine, although a worthy man. The shadows of the Virginia creeper fell on the red pavement, and Kitty's light voice was heard on the staircase. Presently she appeared, and lifting the trailing foliage, she spoke to him. She took him away, and the parson watched the white lines being marked on the sward. He watched them walk by the iron railing that separated Little Leywood from Leywood, the Squire's house. They passed through a small wooden gate into a bit of thick wood, and so gained the drive. Mr Austin took John to see the horses, Kitty ran to see the girls who were in" their room dressing. How they chattered as they came down stairs, and with what lightness and laughter they went to Little Leywood. Their interests were centred in John, and Kitty took the foremost place as an engaged girl. After dinner young men arrived, and tennis was played unceasingly. At six o'clock, tired and hot with air and exercise, all went in to tea—a high tea. At seven John said he must be thinking of getting home; and happy and glad with all the pleasant influences of the day upon them, Kitty and the Miss Austins accompanied him as far as the farm gate.

"What a beautiful walk you will have, Mr Norton; but aren't you tired? Seven miles in the morning and seven in the evening!"

"But I have had the whole day to rest in."

"What a lovely evening! Let's all walk a little way with him," said Kitty.

"I should like to," said the elder Miss Austin, "but we promised father to be home for dinner. The one sure way of getting into his black books is to keep his dinner waiting, and he wouldn't dine without us."

"Well, good-bye, dear," said Kitty, "I shall walk as far as the burgh."

The Miss Austins turned into the rich trees that encircle Leywood, Kitty and John faced the hill. They were soon silhouettes, and ascending, they stood, tiny specks upon the pink evening hours. The table-land swept about them in multitudinous waves; it was silent and solitary as the sea. Lancing College, some miles distant, stood lonely as a lighthouse, and beneath it the Ada flowed white and sluggish through the marshes, the long spine of the skeleton bridge was black, and there, by that low shore, the sea was full of mist, and sea and shore and sky were lost in opal and grey. Old Shoreham, with its air of commerce, of stagnant commerce, stood by the sea. The tide was out, the sea gates were dry, only a few pools flashed silver amid the ooze; and the masts of the tall vessels,—tall vessels aground in that strange canal or rather dyke which runs parallel with and within a few yards of the sea for so many miles,—tapered and. leaned out over the sea banks, and the points of the top masts could be counted. Then on the left hand towards Brighton, the sea streamed with purple, it was striped with green, and it hung like a blue veil behind the rich trees of Leywood and Little Leywood, and the trees and the fields were full of golden rays.

The lovers stood on a grassy plain; sheep were travelling over the great expanses of the valleys; rooks were flying about. Looking over the plain you saw Southwick,—a gleam of gables, a gleam of walls,—skirting a plantation; and further away still, Brighton lay like a pile of rocks heaped about a low shore.

To the lovers life was now as an assortment of simple but beautiful flowers; and they passed the blossoms to and fro and bound them into a bouquet. They talked of the Miss Austins, of their flirtations, of the Rectory, of Thornby Place, of Italy, for there they were going next month on their honeymoon, The turnip and corn lands were as inconceivable widths of green and yellow satin rolling through the rich light of the crests into the richer shadow of the valleys. And there was a farm-house surrounded by buildings, surrounded by trees,—it looked like a nest in its snug hollow; the smoke ascended blue and peacefully. It was the last habitation. Beyond it the downs extend, in almost illimitable ranges ascending to the wild golden gorse, to the purple heather.

We are on the burgh. The hills tumble this way and that; below is the great weald of Sussex, blue with vapour, spotted with gold fields, level as a landscape by Hobbema; Chanctonbury Ring stands up like a gaunt watcher; its crown of trees is pressed upon its brow, a dark and imperial crown.

Overhead the sky is full of dark grey clouds; through them the sun breaks and sheds silver dust over the landscape; in the passing gleams the green of the furze grows vivid. If you listen you hear the tinkling of the bell-wether; if you look you see a solitary rabbit. A stunted hawthorn stands by the circle of stone, and by it the lovers were sitting. He was talking to her of Italy, of cathedrals and statues, for although he now loves her as a man should love, he still saw his honeymoon in a haze of Botticellis, cardinals, and chants. They stood up and bid each other good-bye, and waving hands they parted.

Night was coming on apace, a long way lay still before him, and he walked hastily; she being nearer home, sauntered leisurely, swinging her parasol. The sweetness of the evening was in her blood and brain, and the architectural beauty of the landscape—the elliptical arches of the hills—swam before her. But she had not walked many minutes before a tramp, like a rabbit out of a bush, sprang out of the furze where he had been sleeping. He was a gaunt hulking fellow, six feet high.

"Now 'aven't you a copper or two for a poor fellow, Missie?"

Kitty started from him frightened. "No, I haven't, I have nothing . . . . go away."

He laughed hoarsely, she ran from him. "Now, don't run so fast, Missie, won't you give a poor fellow something?"

"I have nothing."

"Oh, yes you 'ave; what about those pretty lips?"

A few strides brought him again to her side. He laid his hand upon her arm. She broke her parasol across his face, he laughed hoarsely. She saw his savage beast-like eyes fixed hungrily upon her. She fainted for fear of his look of dull tigerish cruelty. She fell . . . .

When shaken and stunned and terrified she rose from the ground, she saw the tall gaunt figure passing away like a shadow. The wild solitary landscape was pale and dim. In the fading light it was a drawing made on blue paper with a hard pencil. The long undulating lines were denned on the dead sky, the girdle of blue encircling sea was an image of eternity. All now was the past, there did not seem to be a present. Her mind was rocked to and fro, and on its surface words and phrases floated like sea weed. . . . To throw her down and ill - treat her. Her frock is spoilt; they will ask her where she has been to, and how she got herself into such a state. Mechanically she brushed herself, and mechanically, very mechanically she picked bits of furze from her dress. She held each away from her and let it drop in a silly vacant way, all the while running the phrases over in her mind: "What a horrible man . . . he threw me down and ill-treated me; my frock is ruined, utterly ruined,

what a state it is in! I had a narrow escape of being murdered. I will tell them that
. . . that will explain . . . I had a narrow escape of being murdered." But presently
she grew conscious that these thoughts were fictitious thoughts, and that there was
a thought, a real thought, lying in the background of her mind, which she dared
not face, which she could not think of, for she did not think as she desired to; her
thoughts came and went at their own wild will, they flitted lightly, touching with
their wings but ever avoiding this deep and formless thought which lay in darkness,
almost undiscoverable, like a monster in a nightmare.

She rose to her feet, she staggered, her sight seemed to fail her. There was
a darkness in the summer evening which she could not account for; the ground
seemed to slide beneath her feet, the landscape seemed to be in motion and to be
rolling in great waves towards the sea. Would it precipitate itself into the sea, and
would she be engulphed in the universal ruin? O! the sea, how implacably serene,
how remorselessly beautiful; green along the shore, purple along the horizon! But
the land was rolling to it. By Lancing College it broke seaward in a soft lapsing tide,
in front of her it rose in angry billows; and Leywood hill, green, and grand, and
voluted, stood up a great green wave against the waveless sea.

"What a horrible man . . . he attacked me, ill-treated me. . . what for?" Her
thoughts turned aside. "He should be put in prison. . . If father knew it, or John
knew it, he would be put in prison, and for a very long time. . . Why did he attack
me? . . . Perhaps to rob me; yes, to rob me, of course to rob me." The evening seemed
to brighten, the tumultuous landscape to grow still, To rob her, and of what? . . . of
her watch; where was it? It was gone. The happiness of a dying saint when he opens
arms to heaven descended upon her. The watch was gone . . . but, had she lost it?
Should she go back and see if she could find it? Oh! impossible; see the place again—
impossible! search among the gorse—impossible! Horror! She would die. O to die
on the lonely hills, to lie stark and cold beneath the stars! But no, she would not be
found upon these hills. She would die and be seen no more. O to die, to sink in that
beautiful sea, so still, so calm, so calm—why would it not take her to its bosom and
hide her away? She would go to it, but she could not get to it; there were thousands
of men between her and it. . . . An icy shiver passed through her.

Then as her thoughts broke away, she thought of how she had escaped being
murdered. How thankful she ought to be—but somehow she is not thankful. And

she was above all things conscious of a horror of returning, of returning to where she would see men and women's faces . . . men's faces. And now with her eyes fixed on the world that awaited her, she stood on the hillside. There was Brighton far away, sparkling in the dying light; nearer, Southwick showed amid woods, winding about the foot of the hills; in front Shoreham rose out of the massy trees of Leywood, the trees slanted down to the lawn and foliage and walls, made spots of white and dark green upon a background of blue sea; further to the right there was a sluggish silver river, the spine of the skeleton bridge, a spur of Lancing hill, and then mist, pale mist, pale grey mist.

"I cannot go home," thought the girl, and acting in direct contradiction to her thoughts, she walked forward. Her parasol—where was it? It was broken. The sheep, how sweet and quiet they looked, and the clover, how deliciously it smelt. . . This is Mr Austin's farm, and how well kept it is. There is the barn. And Evy and Mary, when would they be married? Not so soon as she, she was going to be married in a month. In a month. She repeated the words over to herself; she strove to collect her thoughts, and failing to do so, she walked on hurriedly, she almost ran as if in the motion to force out of sight the thoughts that for a moment threatened to define themselves in her mind. Suddenly she stopped; there were some children playing by the farm gate. They did not know that she was by, and she listened to their childish prattle unsuspected. To listen was an infinite assuagement, one that was overpoweringly sweet, and for some moments she almost forgot. But she woke from her ecstacy in deadly fear and great pain, for coming along the hedgerow the voice of a man was heard, and the children ran away. And she ran too, like a terrified fawn, trembling in every limb, and sick with fear she sped across the meadows. The front door was open; she heard her father calling. To see him she felt would be more than she could bear; she must hide from his sight for ever, and dashing upstairs she double locked her door.

CHAPTER VII.

THE sky was still flushed, there was light upon the sea, but the room was dim and quiet. The room! Kitty had seen it under all aspects, she had lived in it many years: then why does she look with strained eyes? Why does she shrink? Nothing has been changed. There is her little narrow bed, and her little bookcase full of novels and prayer-books; there is her work-basket by the fireplace, by the fireplace closed in with curtains that she herself embroidered; above her pillow there is a crucifix; there are photographs of the Miss Austins, and pictures of pretty children cut from the Christmas Numbers on the walls. She starts at the sight of these familiar objects! She trembles in the room which she thought of as a haven of refuge. Why does she grasp the rail of the bed—why? She scarcely knows: something that is at once remembrance and suspicion fills her mind. Is this her room?

The thought ended. She walked hurriedly to and fro, and as she passed the fuchsia in the window a blossom fell.

She sat down and stared into dark space. She walked languidly and purposelessly to the wardrobe. She stopped to pick a petal from the carpet. The sound of the last door was over, the retiring footfall had died away in the distance, the last voice was hushed; the moon was shining on the sea. A lovely scene, silver and blue; but how the girl's heart was beating! She sighed.

She sighed as if she had forgotten, and approaching her bedside she raised her hands to her neck. It was the instinctive movement of undressing. Her hands dropped, she did not even unbutton her collar. She could not. She resumed her walk, she picked up a blossom that had fallen, she looked out on the pale white sea. There was moonlight now in the room, a ghastly white spot was on the pillow. She was tired. The moonlight called her. She lay down with her profile in the light.

But there were smell and features in the glare—the odour was that of the tramp's skin, the features—a long thin nose, pressed lips, small eyes, a look of dull liquorish cruelty. And this presence was beside her; she could not rid herself of it, she repulsed it with cries, but it came again, and mocking, lay on the pillow.

Horrible, too horrible! She sprang from the bed. Was there anyone in her room? How still it was! The mysterious moonlight, the sea white as a shroud, the sward so chill and death-like. What! Did it move? Was it he? That fearsome shadow! Was she safe? Had they forgotten to bar up the house? Her father's house! Horrible, too horrible, she must shut out this treacherous light—darkness were better. . . .

The curtains are closed, but a ray glinting between the wall and curtain shows her face convulsed. Something follows her: she knows not what, her thoughts are monstrous and obtuse. She dares not look round, she would turn to see if her pursuer is gaining upon her, but some invincible power restrains her. . . . Agony! Her feet catch in, and she falls over great leaves. She falls into the clefts of ruined tombs, and her hands as she attempts to rise are laid on sleeping snakes—rattlesnakes: they turn to attack her, and they glide away and disappear in moss and inscriptions. O, the calm horror of this region! Before her the trees extend in complex colonnades, silent ruins are grown through with giant roots, and about the mysterious entrances of the crypts there lingers yet the odour of ancient sacrifices. The stem of a rare column rises amid the branches, the fragment of an arch hangs over and is supported by a dismantled tree trunk. Ages ago the leaves fell, and withered; ages ago; and now the skeleton arms, lifted in fantastic frenzy against the desert skies, are as weird and symbolic as the hieroglyphics on the tombs below.

And through the torrid twilight of the approaching storm the cry of the hyena is heard.

Flowers hang on every side,—flowers as strange and as gorgeous as Byzantine chalices; flowers narrow and fluted and transparent as long Venetian glasses; opaque flowers bulging and coloured with gold devices like Chinese vases, flowers striped with cinnamon and veined with azure; a million flower-cups and flower chalices, and in these as in censers strange and deadly perfumes are melting, and the heavy fumes descend upon the girl, and they mix with the polluting odour of the ancient sacrifices. She sinks, her arms are raised like those of a victim; she sinks overcome, done to death or worse in some horrible asphyxiation.

And through the torrid twilight of the approaching storm the cry of the hyena is heard. His claws are upon the crumbling tombs.

The suffocating girl utters a thin wail. The vulture pauses, and is stationary on the white and desert skies. She strives with her last strength to free herself from the thrall of the great lianas, and she falls into fresh meshes. . . . The claws are heard amid the ruins, there is a hirsute smell; she turns with terrified eyes to plead, but she meets only the dull liquorish eyes, and the breath of the obscene animal is on her face.

Then she finds herself in the pleasure grounds of Thornby Place. There are the evergreen oaks, there is the rosary flaring all its wealth of red, purple, and white flowers, there is the park encircled by elms, there is the vista filled in with the line of the lofty downs. For a moment she is surprised, and fails to understand. Then she forgets the change of place in new sensations of terror. For across the park something is coming, she knows not what; it will pass her by. She watches a brown and yellow serpent, cubits high. Cubits high. It rears aloft its tawny hide, scenting its prey. The great coiling body, the small head, small as a man's hand, the black bead-like eyes shine out upon the intoxicating blue of the sky. The narrow long head, the fixed black eyes are dull, inexorable desire, conscious of nothing beyond, and only dimly conscious of itself. Will the snake pass by the hiding girl? She rushes to meet it. What folly! She turns and flies.

She takes refuge in the rosary. It follows her, gathering its immense body into horrible and hideous heights. How will she save herself? She will pluck roses, and build a wall between her and it. She collects huge bouquets, armfuls of beautiful flowers, garlands and wreaths. The flower-wall rises, and hoping to combat the fury of the beast with purity, she goes to where beautiful and snowy blossoms grow in clustering millions. She gathers them in haste; her arms and hands are streaming with blood, but she pays no heed, and as the snake surmounts one barricade, she builds another. But in vain. The reptile leans over them all, and the sour dirty smell of the scaly hide befouls the odorous breath of the roses. The long thin neck is upon her; she feels the horrid strength of the coils as they curl and slip about her, drawing her whole life into one knotted and loathsome embrace. And all the while the roses fall in a red and white rain about her. And through the ruin of the roses she escapes from the stench and the coils, and all the while the snake pursues her even into the fountain. The waves and the snake close about her.

Then without any transition in place or time, she finds herself listening to the sound of rippling water. There is an iron drinking cup close to her hand. She seems to recognise the spot. It is Shoreham. There are the streets she knows so well, the masts of the vessels, the downs. But suddenly something darkens the sunlight, the tawny body of the snake oscillates, the people cry to her to escape. She flies along the streets, like the wind she seems to pass. She calls for help. Sometimes the crowds are stationary as if frozen into stone, sometimes they follow the snake and attack it with sticks and knives. One man with colossal shoulders wields a great sabre; it flashes about him like lightning. Will he kill it? He turns and chases a dog, and disappears. The people too have disappeared. She is flying now along a wild plain covered with coarse grass and wild poppies. When she glances behind her she sees the outline of the little coast town, the snake is near her, and there is no one to whom she can call for help. But the sea is in front of her, bound like a blue sash about the cliff's edge. She will escape down the rocks—there is still a chance! The descent is sheer, but somehow she retains foothold. Then the snake drops, she feels his weight upon her, and both fall, fall, fall, and the sea is below them. . . .

With a shriek she sprang from the bed, and still under the influence of the dream, rushed to the window. The moon hung over the sea, the sea flowed with silver, the world was as chill as an icicle.

"The roses, the snake, the cliff's edge, was it then only a dream?" the girl thought. "It was only a dream, a terrible dream, but after all only a dream!" In her hope breathes again, and she smiles like one who thinks he is going to hear that he will not die, but as the old pain returns when the last portion of the deceptive sentence is spoken, so despair came back to her when remembrance pierced the cloud of hallucination, and told her that all was not a dream—there was something that was worse than a dream.

She uttered a low cry, and she moaned. Centuries seemed to have passed, and yet the evil deed remained. It was still night, but what would the day bring to her? There was no hope. Abstract hope from life, and what blank agony you create!

She drew herself up on her bed, and lay with her face buried in the pillow. For the face was beside her: the foul smell was in her nostrils, and the dull, liquorish look of the eyes shone through the darkness. Then sleep came again, and she lay stark and straight as if she were dead, with the light of the moon upon her face. And she sees herself dead. And all her friends are about her crowning her with flowers, beautiful garlands of white roses, and dressing her in a long white robe, white as the snowiest cloud in heaven, and it lies in long straight plaits about her limbs like the robes of those who lie in marble in cathedral aisles. And it falls over her feet, and her hands are crossed over her breast, and all praise in low but ardent words the excessive whiteness of the garment. For none sees but she that there is a black spot upon the robe which they believe to be immaculate. And she would warn them of their error, but she cannot; and when they avert their faces to wipe away their tears, the stain might be easily seen, but when they turn to continue the last offices, folds or flowers have mysteriously fallen over the stain, and hide it from view.

And it is great pain to her to feel herself thus unable to tell them of their error, for she well knows that when she is placed in the tomb, and the angels come, that they will not fail to perceive the stain, and seeing it they will not fail to be shocked and sorrowful,—and seeing it they will turn away weeping, saying, "She is not for us, alas, she is not for us!"

And Kitty, who is conscious of this fatal oversight, the results of which she so clearly foresees, is grievously afflicted, and she makes every effort to warn her friends of their error: but in vain, for there appears to be one amid the mourners who knows that she is endeavouring to announce to them the black stain, and this one whose face she cannot readily distinguish, maliciously and with diabolical ingenuity withdraws attention at the moment when it should fall upon it.

And so it comes that she is buried in the stained robe, and she is carried amid flowers and white cloths to a white marble tomb, where incense is burning, and where the walls are hung with votive wreaths and things commemorative of virginal life and its many lovelinesses. But, strange to say, upon all these, upon the flowers and images alike there is some small stain which none sees but she and the one in shadow, the one whose face she cannot recognise. And although she is nailed fast in her coffin, she sees these stains vividly, and the one whose face she cannot recognise sees them too. And this is certain, for the shadow of the face is sometimes stirred by a horrible laugh.

The mourners go, the evening falls, and the wild sunset floats for a while through the western Heavens; and the cemetery becomes a deep green, and in the wind that blows out of Heaven, the cypresses rock like things sad and mute.

And the blue night comes with stars in her tresses, and out of those stars a legion of angels float softly; their white feet hang out of the blown folds, their wings are pointed to the stars. And from out of the earth, out of the mist, but whence and how it is impossible to say, there come other angels dark of hue and foul smelling. But the white angels carry swords, and they wave these swords, and the scene is reflected in them as in a mirror; and the dark angels cower in a corner of the cemetery, but they do not utterly retire.

And then the tomb is opened, and the white angels enter the tomb. And the coffin is opened, and the girl trembles lest the angels should discover the stain she knew of. But lo! to her great joy they do not see it, and they bear her away through the blue night, past the sacred stars, even within the glory of Paradise. And it is not until one whose face she cannot recognize, and whose presence among the angels of Heaven she cannot comprehend, steals away one of the garlands of white with which she was entwined, that the fatal stain becomes visible. The angels are overcome with a mighty sorrow, and relinquishing their burden, they break into song, and the song they sing is one of grief; and above an accompaniment of spheral music it travels through the spaces of Heaven; and she listens to its wailing echoes as she falls, falls,—falls past the sacred stars to the darkness of terrestrial skies,—falls towards the sea where the dark angels are waiting for her; and as she falls she leans with reverted neck and strives to see their faces, and as she nears them she distinguishes one into whose arms she is going; it is, it is—the . . .

"Save me, save me!" she cried; and bewildered and dazed with the dream, she stared on the room, now chill with summer dawn; the pale light broke over the Shoreham sea, over the lordly downs and rich plantations of Leywood. Again she murmured, it was only a dream, it was only a dream; again a sort of presentiment of happiness spread like light through her mind, and again remembrance came with its cruel truths—there was something that was not a dream, but that was worse than the dream. And then with despair in her heart she sat watching the cold sky turn to blue, the delicate bright blue of morning, and the garden grow into yellow and purple and red. There lay the sea, joyous and sparkling in the light of the mounting sun, and the masts of the vessels at anchor in the long water way. The tapering masts were faint on the shiny sky, and now between them and about them a face seemed to be. Sometimes it was fixed on one, sometimes it flashed like a will o' the wisp, and appeared a little to the right or left of where she had last seen it. It was the face that was now buried in her very soul, and sometimes it passed out of the sky into the morning mist, which still heaved about the edges of the woods; and there she saw something grovelling, crouching, crawling,—a wild beast, or was it a man?

She did not weep, nor did she moan. She sat thinking. She dwelt on the remembrance of the hills and the tramp with strange persistency, and yet no more now than before did she attempt to come to conclusions with her thought; it was vague, she would not define it; she brooded over it sullenly and obtusely. Sometimes her thoughts slipped away from it, but with each returning, a fresh stage was marked in the progress of her nervous despair.

So the hours went by. At eight o'clock the maid knocked at the door. Kitty opened it mechanically, and she fell into the woman's arms, weeping and sobbing passionately. The sight of the female face brought infinite relief; it interrupted the jarred and strained sense of the horrible; the secret affinities of sex quickened within her. The woman's presence filled Kitty with the feelings that the harmlessness of a lamb or a soft bird inspires.

CHAPTER VIII.

"BUT what is it, Miss, what is it? Are you ill? Why, Miss, you haven't taken your things off; you haven't been to bed."

"No, I lay down. . . . I have had frightful dreams—that is all."

"But you must be ill, Miss; you look dreadful, Miss. Shall I tell Mr Hare? Perhaps the doctor had better be sent for."

"No, no; pray say nothing about me. Tell my father that I did not sleep, that I am going to lie down for a little while, that he is not to expect me down for breakfast."

"I really think, Miss, that it would be as well for you to see the doctor."

"No, no, no. I am going to lie down, and I am not to be disturbed."

"Shall I fill the bath, Miss? Shall I leave hot water here, Miss?"

"Bath. . . . Hot water. . ." Kitty repeated the words over as if she were striving to grasp a meaning which was suggested, but which eluded her. Then her face relaxed, the expression was one of pitiful despair, and that expression gave way to a sense of nausea, expressed by a quick contraction of the eyes.

She listened to the splashing of the water, and its echoes were repeated indefinably through her soul.

The maid left the room. Kitty's attention was attracted to her dress. It was torn, it was muddy, there were bits of furze sticking to it. She picked these off, and slowly she commenced settling it: but as she did so, remembrance, accurate and simple recollection of facts, returned to her, and the succession was so complete that the effect was equivalent to a re-enduring of the crime, and with a foreknowledge of it, as if to sharpen its horror and increase the sense of the pollution. The lovely hills, the engirdling sea, the sweet glow of evening—she saw it all again. And as if afraid that her brain, now strained like a body on the rack, would suddenly snap, she threw up her arms, and began to take off her dress, as violently as if she would hush thought in abrupt movements. In a moment she was in stays and petticoat. The delicate and almost girlish arms were disfigured by great bruises. Great black and blue stains were spreading through the skin.

Kitty lifted up her arm: she looked at it in surprise; then in horror she rushed to the door where her dressing gown was hanging, and wrapped herself in it tightly, hid herself in it so that no bit of her flesh could be seen.

She threw herself madly on the bed. She moved, pressing herself against the mattress as if she would rub away, free herself from her loathed self. The sight of her hand was horrible to her, and she covered it over hurriedly.

The maid came up with a tray. The trivial jingle of the cups and plates was another suffering added to the ever increasing stress of mind, and now each memory was accompanied by sensations of physical sickness, of nausea.

She slipped from the bed and locked the door. Again she was alone. An hour passed.

Her father came up. His footsteps on the stairs caused her intolerable anguish. On entering the house she had hated to hear his voice, and now that hatred was intensified a thousandfold. His voice sounded in her ears false, ominous, abominable. She could not have opened the door to him, and the effort required to speak a few words, to say she was tired and wished to be left alone, was so great that it almost cost her reason. It was a great relief to hear him go. She asked herself why she hated to hear his voice, but before she could answer a sudden recollection of the tramp sprang upon her. Her nostrils recalled the smell, and her eyes saw the long, thin nose and the dull liquorish eyes beside her on the pillow.

She got up and walked about the room, and its appearance contrasted with and aggravated the fierceness of the fever of passion and horror that raged within her. The homeliness of the teacups and the plates, the tin bath, painted yellow and white, so grotesque and so trim.

But not its water nor even the waves of the great sea would wash away remembrance. She pressed her face against the pane. The wide sea, so peaceful, so serene!

Oblivion, oblivion, O for the waters of oblivion!

Then for an hour she almost forgot; sometimes she listened, and the shrill singing of the canary was mixed with thoughts of her dead brothers and sisters, of her mother. She was waked from her reveries by the farm bell ringing the labourers' dinner hour.

Night had been fearsome with darkness and dreams, but the genial sunlight and the continuous externality of the daytime acted on her mind, and turned vague thoughts, as it were, into sentences, printed in clear type. She often thought she was dead, and she favoured this idea, but she was never wholly dead. She was a lost soul wandering on those desolate hills, the gloom descending, and Brighton and Southwick and Shoreham and Worthing gleaming along the sea banks of a purple sea. There were phantoms—there were two phantoms. One turned to reality, and she walked by her lover's side, talking of Italy. Then he disappeared, and she shrank from the horrible tramp; then both men grew confused in her mind, and in despair she threw herself on her bed. Raising her eyes she caught sight of her prayer-book, but she turned from it moaning, for her misery was too deep for prayer.

The lunch bell rang. She listened to the footsteps on the staircase; she begged to be excused, and she refused to open the door.

The day grew into afternoon. She awoke from a dreamless sleep of about an hour, and still under its soothing influence, she pinned up her hair, settled the ribbons of her dressing gown, and went downstairs. She found her father and John in the drawing-room.

"Oh, here is Kitty!" they exclaimed.

"But what is the matter, dear? Why are you not dressed?" said Mr Hare. "But what is the matter. . . . Are you ill \ "said John, and he extended his hand.

"No, no, 'tis nothing," she replied, and avoiding the outstretched hand with a shudder, she took the seat furthest away from her father and lover.

They looked at her in amazement, and she at them in fear and trembling. She was conscious of two very distinct sensations—one the result of reason, the other of madness. She was not ignorant of the causes of each, although she was powerless to repress one in favour of the other. Both struggled for mastery and for the moment without disturbing the equipoise. On the side of reason she knew very well she was looking at and talking to her dear, kind father, and that the young man sitting next him was John Norton, the son of her clear friend, Mrs Norton; she knew he was the young man who loved her, and whom she was going to marry, marry, marry. On the other side she saw that her father's kind benign countenance was not a real face, but a mask which he wore over another face, and which, should the mask slip—and she prayed that it might not—would prove as horrible and revolting as—

But the mask John wore was as nothing, it was the veriest make believe. And she could not but doubt now but that the face she had known him so long by was a fictitious face, and as the hallucination strengthened, she saw his large mild eyes grow small, and that vague dreamy look turn to the dull liquorish look, the chin came forward, the brows contracted . . . the large sinewy hands were, oh, so like! Then reason asserted itself; the vision vanished, and she saw John Norton as she had always seen him.

But was she sure that she did? Yes, yes—she must not give way. But her head seemed to be growing lighter, and she did not appear to be able to judge things exactly as she should; a sort of new world seemed to be slipping like a painted veil between her and the old. She must resist.

John and Mr Hare looked at her.

John at length rose, and advancing to her, said, "My dear Kitty, I am afraid you are not well. . ."

She strove to allow him to take her hand, but she could not overcome the instinctive feeling which, against her will, caused her to shrink from him.

"Oh, don't come near me, I cannot bear it!" she cried, "don't come near me, I beg of you."

More than this she could not do, and giving way utterly, she shrieked and rushed from the room. She rushed upstairs. She stood in the middle of the floor listening to the silence, her thoughts falling about her like shaken leaves. It was as if a thunderbolt had destroyed the world, and left her alone in a desert. The furniture of the room, the bed, the chairs, the books she loved, seemed to have become as grains of sand, and she forgot all connection between them and herself. She pressed her hands to her forehead, and strove to separate the horror that crowded upon her. But all was now one horror—the lonely hills were in the room, the grey sky, the green furze, the tramp; she was again fighting furiously with him; and her lover and her father and all sense of the world's life grew dark in the storm of madness. Suddenly she felt something on her neck. She put her hand up . . .

And now with madness on her face she caught up a pair of scissors and cut off her hair: one after the other the great tresses of gold and brown fell, until the floor was strewn with them.

A step was heard on the stairs; her quick ears caught the sound, and she rushed to the door to lock it. But she was too late. John held it fast.

"Kitty, Kitty," he cried, "for God's sake, tell me what is the matter!"

"Save me! save me!" she cried, and she forced the door against him with her whole strength. He was, however, determined on questioning her, on seeing her, and he passed his head and shoulders into the room. His heart quailed at the face he saw.

For now had gone that imperceptible something which divides the life of the sane from that of the insane, and he who had so long feared lest a woman might soil the elegant sanctity of his life, disappeared forever from the mind of her whom he had learned to love, and existed to her only as the foul dull brute who had outraged her on the hills.

"Save me, save me! help, help!" she cried, retreating from him.

"Kitty, Kitty, what do you mean? Say, say—"

"Save me; oh mercy, mercy! Let me go, and I will never say I saw you, I will not tell anything. Let me go!" she cried, retreating towards the window.

"For Heaven's sake, Kitty, take care—the window, the window!"

But Kitty heard nothing, knew nothing, was conscious of nothing but a mad desire to escape. The window was lifted high—high above her head, and her face distorted with fear, she stood amid the soft greenery of the Virginia creeper.

"Save me," she cried, "mercy, mercy!"

"Kitty, Kitty darling!"

The white dress passed through the green leaves. John heard a dull thud.

CHAPTER IX.

AND the pity of it! The poor white thing lying like a shot dove, bleeding, and the dreadful blood flowing over the red tiles. . . .

Mr Hare was kneeling by his daughter when John, rushing forth, stopped and stood aghast.

"What is this? Say—speak, speak man, speak; how did this happen?

"I cannot say, I do not know; she did not seem to know me; she ran away. Oh my God, I do not understand; she seemed as if afraid of me, and she threw herself out of the window. But she is not dead. . ."

The word rang out in the silence, ruthlessly brutal in its significance. Mr Hare looked up, his face a symbol of agony. "Oh, dead, how can you speak so. . ."

John felt his being sink and fade like a breath, and then, conscious of nothing, he helped to lift Kitty from the tiles. But it was her father who carried her upstairs. The blood flowed from the terrible wound in the head. Dripped. The walls were stained. When she was laid upon the bed, the pillow was crimson; and the maid-servant coming in, strove to staunch the wound with towels. Kitty did not move.

Both men knew there was no hope. The maidservant retired, and she did not close the door, nor did she ask if the doctor should be sent for. One man held the bed rail, looking at his dead daughter; the other sat by the window. That one was John Norton. His brain was empty, everything was far away. He saw things moving, moving, but they were all so far away. He could not re - knit himself with the weft of life; the thread that had made him part of it had been snapped, and he was left struggling in space. He knew that Kitty had thrown herself out of the window and was dead. The word shocked him a little, but there was no sense of realisation to meet it. She had walked with him on the hills, she had accompanied him as far as the burgh; she had waved her hand to him before they walked quite out of each other's sight. They had been speaking of Italy . . . of Italy where they would have spent their honeymoon. Now she was dead! There would be no honeymoon, no wife. How unreal, how impossible it all did seem, and yet it was real, yes, real enough. There she lay dead; here is her room, and there is her book-case; there are the photographs of the Miss Austins, here is the fuchsia with the pendent blossoms falling, and her canary is singing. John glanced at the cage, and the song Went to his brain, and he was horrified, for there was no grief in his heart.

Had he not loved her? Yes, he was sure of that; then why was there no burning grief nor any tears? He envied the hard-sobbing father's grief, the father who, prostrate by the bedside, held his dead daughter's hand, and showed a face wild with fear—a face on which was printed so deeply the terror of the soul's emotion, that John felt a supernatural awe creep upon him; felt that his presence was a sort of sacrilege. He crept downstairs. He went into the drawing-room, and looked about for the place he had last seen her in. There it was. . . . There. But his eyes wandered from the place, for it was there he had seen the startled face, the half mad face which he had seen afterwards at the window, quite mad.

On that sofa she usually sat; how often had he seen her sitting there! And now he would not see her any more. And only three days ago she had been sitting in the basket chair. How well he remembered her words, her laughter, and now . . . now; was it possible he never would hear her laugh again? How frail a thing is human life, how shadow-like; one moment it is here, the next it is gone. Here is her work-basket; and here the very ball of wool which he had held for her to wind; and here is a novel which she had lent to him, and which he had forgotten to take away. He would never read it now; or perhaps he should read it in memory of her, of her whom yesterday he parted with on the hills,—her little puritan look, her external girlishness, her golden brown hair and the sudden laugh so characteristic of her. . . . She had lent him this book—she who was now but clay; she who was to have been his wife. His wife! The thought struck him. Now he would never have a wife. What was there for him to do? To turn his house into a Gothic monastery, and himself into a monk. Very horrible and very bitter in its sheer grotesqueness was the thought. It was as if in one moment he saw the whole of his life summarised in a single symbol, and understood its vanity and its folly. Ah, there was nothing for him, no wife, no life. . . . The tears welled up in his eyes; the shock which in its suddenness had frozen his heart, began to thaw, and grief fell like a penetrating rain.

We learn to suffer as we learn to love, and it is not to-day, nor yet to-morrow, but in weeks and months to come, and by slow degrees, that John Norton will understand the irreparableness of his loss. There is a man upstairs who crouches like stone by his dead daughter's side; he is motionless and pale as the dead, he is as great in his grief as an expression of grief by Michael Angelo. The hours pass, he is unconscious of them; he sees not the light dying on the sea, he hears not the trilling of the canary. He knows of nothing but his dead child, and that the world would be nothing to give to have her speak to him once again. His is the humblest and the worthiest sorrow, but such sorrow cannot affect John Norton. He has dreamed too much and reflected too much on the meaning of life; his suffering is too original in himself, too self-centred, and at the same time too much based on the inherent misery of existence, to allow him to project himself into and suffer with any individual grief, no matter how nearly it might be allied to him and to his personal interest. He knew his weakness in this direction, and now he gladly welcomed the coming of grief, for indeed he had felt not a little shocked at the aridness of his heart, and frightened lest his eyes should remain dry even to the end.

Suddenly he remembered that the Miss Austins had said that they would call to-morrow early for Kitty, to take her to Leywood to lunch. . . . They were going to have some tennis in the afternoon. He too was expected there. They must be told what had occurred. It would be terrible if they came calling for Kitty under her window, and she lying dead! This slight incident in the tragedy wrung his heart, and the effort of putting the facts upon paper brought the truth home to him, and lured and led him to see down the lifelong range of consequences. The doctor too, he thought, must be warned of what had happened. And with the letter telling the sad story in his hand, and illimitable sorrow in his soul, he went out in the evening air. It was just such an evening as yester evening—a little softer, a little lovelier, perhaps; earth, sea, and sky appeared like an exquisite vision upon whose lips there is fragrance, yet in whose eyes a glow of passion still survives.

The beauty of the last hour of light is upon that crescent of sea, and the ships loll upon the long strand, the tapering masts and slacking ropes vanish upon the pallid sky. There is the old town, dusty, and dreamy, and brown, with neglected wharfs and quays; there is the new town, vulgar and fresh with green paint and trees, and looking hungrily on the broad lands of the Squire, the broad lands and the rich woods which rise up the hill side to the barn on the limit of the clowns. How beautiful the great green woods look as they sweep up a small expanse of the downs, like a wave over a slope of sand. And there is a house with red gables where the girls are still on the tennis lawn. John walked through the town; he told the doctor he must go at once to the rectory. He walked to Leywood and left his letter with the lodge-keeper; and then, as if led by a strange fascination, he passed through the farm gate and set out to return home across the hills.

"She was here with me yesterday; how beautiful she looked, and how graceful were her laughter and speech," he said, turning suddenly and looking down on the landscape; on the massy trees contrasting with the walls of the town, the spine-like bridge crossing the marshy shore, the sails of the mill turning over the crest of the hill. The night was falling fast, as a blue veil it hung down over the sea, but the deep pure sky seemed in one spot to grow clear, and suddenly the pale moon shone and shimmered upon the sea. The landscape gained in loveliness, the sheep seemed like phantoms, the solitary barns like monsters of the night. And the hills were like giants sleeping, and the long outlines were prolonged far away into the depths and mistiness of space. Turning again and looking through a vista in the hills, John could see Brighton, a pale cloud of fire, set by the moon-illumined sea, and nearer was Southwick, grown into separate lines of light, that wandered into and lost themselves among the outlying hollows of the hills; and below him and in front of him Shoreham lay, a blaze of living fire, a thousand lights; lights everywhere save in one gloomy spot, and there John knew that his beloved was lying dead. And further away, past the shadowy marshy shores, was Worthing, the palest of nebulæ in these earthly constellations; and overhead the stars of heaven shone as if in pitiless disdain. The blown hawthorn bush that stands by the burgh leaned out, a ship sailed slowly across the rays of the moon. Yesterday they parted here in the glad golden sunlight, parted for ever, for ever.

"Yesterday I had all things—a sweet wife and happy youthful clays to look forward to. To-day I have nothing; all my hopes are shattered, all my illusions have fallen. So is it always with him who places his trust in life. Ah, life, life, what hast thou for giving save cruel deceptions and miserable wrongs? Ah, why did I leave my life of contemplation and prayer to enter into that of desire. . . Ah, I knew, well I knew there was no happiness save in calm and contemplation. Ah, well I knew; and she is gone, gone, gone!"

We suffer differently indeed, but we suffer equally. The death of his sweetheart forces one man to reflect anew on the slightness of life's pleasures and the depth of life's griefs. In the peaceful valley of natural instincts and affections he had slept for a while, now he awoke on one of the high peaks lit with the rays of intense consciousness, and he cried aloud, and withdrew in terror at a too vivid realisation of self. The other man wept for the daughter that had gone out of his life, wept for her pretty face and cheerful laughter, wept for her love, wept for the years he would live without her. We know which sorrow is the manliest, which appeals to our sympathy, but who can measure the depth of John Norton's suffering? It was as vast as the night, cold as the stream of moonlit sea.

He did not arrive home till late, and having told his mother what had happened, he instantly retired to his room. Dreams followed him. The hills were in his dreams. There were enemies there; he was often pursued by savages, and he often saw Kitty captured; nor could he ever evade their wandering vigilance and release her. Again and again he awoke, and remembered that she was dead.

Next morning John and Mrs Norton drove to the rectory, and without asking for Mr Hare, they went up to *her* room. The windows were open, and Annie and Mary Austin sat by the bedside watching. The blood had been washed out of the beautiful hair, and she lay very white and fair amid the roses her friends had brought her. She lay as she had lain in one of her terrible dreams—quite still, the slender body covered by a sheet, moulding it with sculptured delight and love. From the feet the linen curved and marked the inflections of the knees; there were long flowing folds, low-lying like the wash of retiring water; the rounded shoulders, the neck, the calm and bloodless face, the little nose, and the beautiful drawing of the nostrils, the extraordinary waxen pallor, the eyelids laid like rose leaves upon the eyes that death has closed for ever. Within the arm, in the pale hand extended, a great Eucharis lily had been laid, its carved blossoms bloomed in unchanging stillness, and the whole scene was like a sad dream in the whitest marble.

Candles were burning, and the soft smell of wax mixed with the perfume of the roses. For there were roses everywhere—great snowy bouquets, and long lines of scattered blossoms, and single roses there and here, and petals fallen and falling were as tears shed for the beautiful dead, and the white flowerage vied with the pallor and the immaculate stillness of the dead.

The calm chastity, the lonely loveliness, so sweetly removed from taint of passion, struck John with all the emotion of art. He reproached himself for having dreamed of her rather as a wife than as a sister, and then all art and all conscience went down as a broken wreck in the wild washing sea of deep human love: he knelt by her bedside, and sobbed piteously, a man whose life is broken.

When they next saw her she was in her coffin. It was almost full of white blossoms—jasmine, Eucharis lilies, white roses, and in the midst of the flowers you saw the hands folded, and the face was veiled with some delicate filmy handkerchief.

For the funeral there were crosses and wreaths of white flowers, roses and stephanotis. And the Austin girls and their cousins who had come from Brighton and Worthing carried loose flowers. How black and sad, how homely and humble they seemed. Down the short drive, through the iron gate, through the farm gate, the bearers staggering a little under the weight of lead, the little cortége passed two by two. A broken-hearted lover, a grief-stricken father, and a dozen sweet girls, their eyes and cheeks streaming with tears. Kitty, their girl-friend was dead, dead, dead! The words rang in their hearts in answer to the mournful tolling of the bell. The little by-way along which they went, the little green path leading over the hill, under trees shot through and through with the whiteness of summer seas, was strewn with blossoms fallen from the bier and the dolent fingers of the weeping girls.

The old church was all in white; great lilies in vases, wreaths of stephanotis; and, above all, roses—great garlands of white roses had been woven, and they hung along and across. A blossom fell, a sob sounded in the stillness; and how trivial it all seemed, and how impotent to assuage the bitter burning of human sorrow: how paltry and circumscribed the old grey church, with its little graveyard full of forgotten griefs and aspirations! This hour of beautiful sorrow and roses, how long will it be remembered? The coffin sinks out of sight, out of sight for ever, a snowdrift of delicate bloom descending into the earth.

CHAPTER X.

FROM the Austin girls, whose eyes followed him, from Mr Hare, from Mrs Norton, John wandered sorrowfully away,—he wandered through the green woods and fields into the town. He stood by the railway gates. He saw the people coming and going in and out of the public houses; and he watched the trains that whizzed past, and he understood nothing, not even why the great bar of the white gate did not yield beneath the pressure of his hands; and in the great vault of the blue sky, white clouds melted and faded to sheeny visions of paradise, to a white form with folded wings, and eyes whose calm was immortality. . . .

A train stopped. He took a ticket and went to Brighton. As they steamed along a high embankment, he found himself looking into a little suburban cemetery. The graves, the yews, the sharp church spire touching the range of the hills. *Earth to earth, ashes to ashes, dust to dust,* and the dread responsive rattle given back by the coffin lid. He watched the group in the distant corner, and its very remoteness and removal from his personal knowledge and concern, moved him to passionate grief and tears. . .

He walked through the southern sunlight of the town to the long expanse of sea. The mundane pier is taut and trim, and gay with the clangour of the band, the brown sails of the fishing boats wave in the translucid greens of water; and the white field of the sheer cliff, and all the roofs, gables, spires, balconies, and the green of the verandahs are exquisitely indicated and elusive in the bright air; and the beach is strange with acrobats and comic songs, nursemaids lying on the pebbles reading novels, children with their clothes tied tightly about them building sand castles zealously; see the lengthy crowd of promenaders—out of its ranks two little spots of mauve come running to meet the advancing wave, and now they fly back again, and now they come again frolicking like butterflies, as gay and as bright.

Under the impulse of his ravening grief, John watched the spectacle of the world's forgetfulness, and the seeming obscenity horrified him even to the limits of madness. He cried that it might pass from him. Solitude—the solemn peace of the hills, the appealing silence of a pine wood at even; how holy is the idea of solitude, find it where you will. The Gothic pile, the apostles and saints of the windows, the deep purples and crimsons, and the sunlight streaming through, and the pathetic responses and the majesty of the organ do not take away, but enhance and affirm the sensation of idea and God. The quiet rooms austere with Latin and crucifix; John could see them. Fondly he allowed these fancies to linger, but through the dream a sense of reality began to grow, and he remembered the narrowness of the life, when viewed from the material side, and its necessary promiscuousness, and he thought with horror of the impossibility of the preservation of that personal life, with all its sanctuary-like intensity, which was so dear to him. He waved away all thought of priesthood, and walking quickly down the pier, looking on the gay panorama of town and beach, he said, "The world shall be my monastery."

THE END

The Codes Of Hammurabi And Moses
W. W. Davies

QTY

The discovery of the Hammurabi Code is one of the greatest achievements of archaeology, and is of paramount interest, not only to the student of the Bible, but also to all those interested in ancient history...

Religion   **ISBN: *1-59462-338-4***   **Pages:132**
MSRP $12.95

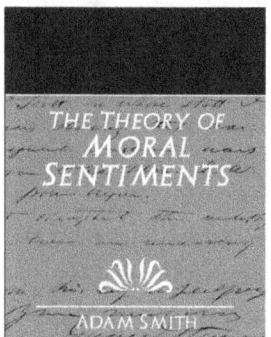

The Theory of Moral Sentiments
Adam Smith

QTY

This work from 1749. contains original theories of conscience amd moral judgment and it is the foundation for systemof morals.

Philosophy   ISBN: *1-59462-777-0*   **Pages:536**
MSRP $19.95

Jessica's First Prayer
Hesba Stretton

QTY

In a screened and secluded corner of one of the many railway-bridges which span the streets of London there could be seen a few years ago, from five o'clock every morning until half past eight, a tidily set-out coffee-stall, consisting of a trestle and board, upon which stood two large tin cans, with a small fire of charcoal burning under each so as to keep the coffee boiling during the early hours of the morning when the work-people were thronging into the city on their way to their daily toil...

Childrens   ISBN: *1-59462-373-2*   **Pages:84**
MSRP $9.95

My Life and Work
Henry Ford

QTY

Henry Ford revolutionized the world with his implementation of mass production for the Model T automobile. Gain valuable business insight into his life and work with his own auto-biography... "We have only started on our development of our country we have not as yet, with all our talk of wonderful progress, done more than scratch the surface. The progress has been wonderful enough but..."

Pages:300

Biographies/   ISBN: *1-59462-198-5*   *MSRP $21.95*

The Art of Cross-Examination
Francis Wellman

QTY

I presume it is the experience of every author, after his first book is published upon an important subject, to be almost overwhelmed with a wealth of ideas and illustrations which could readily have been included in his book, and which to his own mind, at least, seem to make a second edition inevitable. Such certainly was the case with me; and when the first edition had reached its sixth impression in five months, I rejoiced to learn that it seemed to my publishers that the book had met with a sufficiently favorable reception to justify a second and considerably enlarged edition. ..

Pages:412

Reference   ISBN: *1-59462-647-2*   *MSRP $19.95*

On the Duty of Civil Disobedience
Henry David Thoreau

QTY

Thoreau wrote his famous essay, On the Duty of Civil Disobedience, as a protest against an unjust but popular war and the immoral but popular institution of slave-owning. He did more than write—he declined to pay his taxes, and was hauled off to gaol in consequence. Who can say how much this refusal of his hastened the end of the war and of slavery ?

Law   ISBN: *1-59462-747-9*   **Pages:48**

MSRP $7.45

Dream Psychology Psychoanalysis for Beginners
Sigmund Freud

QTY

Sigmund Freud, born Sigismund Schlomo Freud (May 6, 1856 - September 23, 1939), was a Jewish-Austrian neurologist and psychiatrist who co-founded the psychoanalytic school of psychology. Freud is best known for his theories of the unconscious mind, especially involving the mechanism of repression; his redefinition of sexual desire as mobile and directed towards a wide variety of objects; and his therapeutic techniques, especially his understanding of transference in the therapeutic relationship and the presumed value of dreams as sources of insight into unconscious desires.

Dream Psychology
Psychoanalysis for Beginners

Sigmund Freud

Pages:196

Psychology   ISBN: *1-59462-905-6*   *MSRP $15.45*

The Miracle of Right Thought
Orison Swett Marden

QTY

Believe with all of your heart that you will do what you were made to do. When the mind has once formed the habit of holding cheerful, happy, prosperous pictures, it will not be easy to form the opposite habit. It does not matter how improbable or how far away this realization may see, or how dark the prospects may be, if we visualize them as best we can, as vividly as possible, hold tenaciously to them and vigorously struggle to attain them, they will gradually become actualized, realized in the life. But a desire, a longing without endeavor, a yearning abandoned or held indifferently will vanish without realization.

Pages:360

Self Help   ISBN: *1-59462-644-8*   *MSRP $25.45*

The Rosicrucian Cosmo-Conception Mystic Christianity by *Max Heindel*   ISBN: *1-59462-188-8*   **$38.95**
The Rosicrucian Cosmo-conception is not dogmatic, neither does it appeal to any other authority than the reason of the student. It is: not controversial, but is: sent forth in the, hope that it may help to clear..   *New Age/Religion Pages 646*

Abandonment To Divine Providence by *Jean-Pierre de Caussade*   ISBN: *1-59462-228-0*   **$25.95**
"The Rev. Jean Pierre de Caussade was one of the most remarkable spiritual writers in France in the 18th Century. His death took place at Toulouse in 1751. His works have gone through many editions and have been republished...   *Inspirational/Religion Pages 400*

Mental Chemistry by *Charles Haanel*   ISBN: *1-59462-192-6*   **$23.95**
Mental Chemistry allows the change of material conditions by combining and appropriately utilizing the power of the mind. Much like applied chemistry creates something new and unique out of careful combinations of chemicals the mastery of mental chemistry...   *New Age/Business Pages 354*

The Letters of Robert Browning and Elizabeth Barret Barrett 1845-1846 vol II   ISBN: *1-59462-193-4*   **$35.95**
by *Robert Browning* and *Elizabeth Barrett*   *Biographies Pages 596*

Gleanings In Genesis (volume I) by *Arthur W. Pink*   ISBN: *1-59462-130-6*   **$27.45**
Appropriately has Genesis been termed "the seed plot of the Bible" for in it we have, in germ form, almost all of the great doctrines which are afterwards fully developed in the books of Scripture which follow...   *Religion/Inspirational Pages 420*

The Master Key by *L. W. de Laurence*   ISBN: *1-59462-001-6*   **$30.95**
In no branch of human knowledge has there been a more lively increase of the spirit of research during the past few years than in the study of Psychology, Concentration and Mental Discipline. The requests for authentic lessons in Thought Control, Mental Discipline and...   *New Age/Business Pages 422*

The Lesser Key Of Solomon Goetia by *L. W. de Laurence*   ISBN: *1-59462-092-X*   **$9.95**
This translation of the first book of the "Lernegton" which is now for the first time made accessible to students of Talismanic Magic was done, after careful collation and edition, from numerous Ancient Manuscripts in Hebrew, Latin, and French...   *New Age/Occult Pages 92*

Rubaiyat Of Omar Khayyam by *Edward Fitzgerald*   ISBN:*1-59462-332-5*   **$13.95**
Edward Fitzgerald, whom the world has already learned, in spite of his own efforts to remain within the shadow of anonymity, to look upon as one of the rarest poets of the century, was born at Bredfield, in Suffolk, on the 31st of March, 1809. He was the third son of John Purcell...   *Music Pages 172*

Ancient Law by *Henry Maine*   ISBN: *1-59462-128-4*   **$29.95**
The chief object of the following pages is to indicate some of the earliest ideas of mankind, as they are reflected in Ancient Law, and to point out the relation of those ideas to modern thought.   *Religion/History Pages 452*

Far-Away Stories by *William J. Locke*   ISBN: *1-59462-129-2*   **$19.45**
"Good wine needs no bush, but a collection of mixed vintages does. And this book is just such a collection. Some of the stories I do not want to remain buried for ever in the museum files of dead magazine-numbers an author's not unpardonable vanity..."   *Fiction Pages 272*

Life of David Crockett by *David Crockett*   ISBN: *1-59462-250-7*   **$27.45**
"Colonel David Crockett was one of the most remarkable men of the times in which he lived. Born in humble life, but gifted with a strong will, an indomitable courage, and unremitting perseverance...   *Biographies/New Age Pages 424*

Lip-Reading by *Edward Nitchie*   ISBN: *1-59462-206-X*   **$25.95**
Edward B. Nitchie, founder of the New York School for the Hard of Hearing, now the Nitchie School of Lip-Reading, Inc, wrote "LIP-READING Principles and Practice". The development and perfecting of this meritorious work on lip-reading was an undertaking...   *How-to Pages 400*

A Handbook of Suggestive Therapeutics, Applied Hypnotism, Psychic Science   ISBN: *1-59462-214-0*   **$24.95**
by *Henry Munro*   *Health/New Age/Health/Self-help Pages 376*

A Doll's House: and Two Other Plays by *Henrik Ibsen*   ISBN: *1-59462-112-8*   **$19.95**
Henrik Ibsen created this classic when in revolutionary 1848 Rome. Introducing some striking concepts in playwriting for the realist genre, this play has been studied the world over.   *Fiction/Classics/Plays 308*

The Light of Asia by *sir Edwin Arnold*   ISBN: *1-59462-204-3*   **$13.95**
In this poetic masterpiece, Edwin Arnold describes the life and teachings of Buddha. The man who was to become known as Buddha to the world was born as Prince Gautama of India but he rejected the worldly riches and abandoned the reigns of power when...   *Religion/History/Biographies Pages 170*

The Complete Works of Guy de Maupassant by *Guy de Maupassant*   ISBN: *1-59462-157-8*   **$16.95**
"For days and days, nights and nights, I had dreamed of that first kiss which was to consecrate our engagement, and I knew not on what spot I should put my lips..."   *Fiction/Classics Pages 240*

The Art of Cross-Examination by *Francis L. Wellman*   ISBN: *1-59462-309-0*   **$26.95**
Written by a renowned trial lawyer, Wellman imparts his experience and uses case studies to explain how to use psychology to extract desired information through questioning.   *How-to/Science/Reference Pages 408*

Answered or Unanswered? by *Louisa Vaughan*   ISBN: *1-59462-248-5*   **$10.95**
Miracles of Faith in China   *Religion Pages 112*

The Edinburgh Lectures on Mental Science (1909) by *Thomas*   ISBN: *1-59462-008-3*   **$11.95**
This book contains the substance of a course of lectures recently given by the writer in the Queen Street Hail, Edinburgh. Its purpose is to indicate the Natural Principles governing the relation between Mental Action and Material Conditions...   *New Age/Psychology Pages 148*

Ayesha by *H. Rider Haggard*   ISBN: *1-59462-301-5*   **$24.95**
Verily and indeed it is the unexpected that happens! Probably if there was one person upon the earth from whom the Editor of this, and of a certain previous history, did not expect to hear again...   *Classics Pages 380*

Ayala's Angel by *Anthony Trollope*   ISBN: *1-59462-352-X*   **$29.95**
The two girls were both pretty, but Lucy who was twenty-one who supposed to be simple and comparatively unattractive, whereas Ayala was credited, as her Bombwhat romantic name might show, with poetic charm and a taste for romance. Ayala when her father died was nineteen...   *Fiction Pages 484*

The American Commonwealth by *James Bryce*   ISBN: *1-59462-286-8*   **$34.45**
An interpretation of American democratic political theory. It examines political mechanics and society from the perspective of Scotsman James Bryce   *Politics Pages 572*

Stories of the Pilgrims by *Margaret P. Pumphrey*   ISBN: *1-59462-116-0*   **$17.95**
This book explores pilgrims religious oppression in England as well as their escape to Holland and eventual crossing to America on the Mayflower, and their early days in New England...   *History Pages 268*

QTY

The Fasting Cure *by Sinclair Upton*   ISBN: *1-59462-222-1* **$13.95**
In the Cosmopolitan Magazine for May, 1910, and in the Contemporary Review (London) for April, 1910, I published an article dealing with my experiences in fasting. I have written a great many magazine articles, but never one which attracted so much attention... New Age/Self Help/Health Pages 164

Hebrew Astrology *by Sepharial*   ISBN: *1-59462-308-2* **$13.45**
In these days of advanced thinking it is a matter of common observation that we have left many of the old landmarks behind and that we are now pressing forward to greater heights and to a wider horizon than that which represented the mind-content of our progenitors... Astrology Pages 144

Thought Vibration or The Law of Attraction in the Thought World   ISBN: *1-59462-127-6* **$12.95**
by William Walker Atkinson   Psychology/Religion Pages 144

Optimism *by Helen Keller*   ISBN: *1-59462-108-X* **$15.95**
Helen Keller was blind, deaf, and mute since 19 months old, yet famously learned how to overcome these handicaps, communicate with the world, and spread her lectures promoting optimism. An inspiring read for everyone... Biographies/Inspirational Pages 84

Sara Crewe *by Frances Burnett*   ISBN: *1-59462-360-0* **$9.45**
In the first place, Miss Minchin lived in London. Her home was a large, dull, tall one, in a large, dull square, where all the houses were alike, and all the sparrows were alike, and where all the door-knockers made the same heavy sound... Childrens/Classic Pages 88

The Autobiography of Benjamin Franklin *by Benjamin Franklin*   ISBN: *1-59462-135-7* **$24.95**
The Autobiography of Benjamin Franklin has probably been more extensively read than any other American historical work, and no other book of its kind has had such ups and downs of fortune. Franklin lived for many years in England, where he was agent... Biographies/History Pages 332

Name	
Email	
Telephone	
Address	
City, State ZIP	

☐ Credit Card   ☐ Check / Money Order

Credit Card Number	
Expiration Date	
Signature	

Please Mail to: Book Jungle
PO Box 2226
Champaign, IL 61825
or Fax to: 630-214-0564

ORDERING INFORMATION

web: *www.bookjungle.com*
email: *sales@bookjungle.com*
fax: *630-214-0564*
mail: *Book Jungle PO Box 2226 Champaign, IL 61825*
or PayPal *to sales@bookjungle.com*

Please contact us for bulk discounts

DIRECT-ORDER TERMS

**20% Discount if You Order
Two or More Books**
Free Domestic Shipping!
Accepted: Master Card, Visa,
Discover, American Express

www.ingramcontent.com/pod-product-compliance
Lightning Source LLC
Chambersburg PA
CBHW081004280626
47160CB00017B/2927